8/87

ALSO BY SUSAN TROTT

*The Housewife and the Assassin*

*When Your Lover Leaves...*

*Incognito*

*Don't Tell Laura*

# SUSAN TROTT

SIMON AND SCHUSTER

NEW YORK

This novel is a work of fiction. Names, places, and incidents either are the product of the author's imagination or are used fictitiously. Any resemblance to actual events or locales is entirely coincidental. All the characters in this story are wholly imaginary except for Ernest Hemingway, whom I never knew, and Count Felix Von Luckner, whom I did.

The journal excerpts in chapter 22 are from the 1917 journal of my father, Emery Trott.

Copyright © 1987 by Susan Trott
All rights reserved
including the right of reproduction
in whole or in part in any form
Published by Simon and Schuster
A Division of Simon & Schuster, Inc.
Simon & Schuster Building
Rockefeller Center
1230 Avenue of the Americas
New York, New York 10020
SIMON AND SCHUSTER and colophon are registered trademarks of
Simon & Schuster, Inc.

Designed by Levavi & Levavi, Inc.
Manufactured in the United States of America

10  9  8  7  6  5  4  3  2  1

Library of Congress Cataloging-in-Publication Data
Trott, Susan.
  Sightings.

  I. Title.
PS3570.R594S5    1987       813'.54       87-4264

ISBN: 0-671-63804-1

*To my magnificent children:*
*Ann, Emery, and Natalie Mitchell. Thank you.*

SIGHTINGS

# 1. PARIS, FRANCE

$\mathbf{M}$y mother adored my father. So did I. He was a famous man but also a nice man. As a high school graduation present he sent me to Paris and that's where I was, age eighteen, when I heard he had run away with my friend Chris, a girl my age, exactly—my best friend, who I'd known since kindergarten! And what about Mom, who adored him? She ran away too. First!

When Daddy's call came, I was in bed with Masefield, a spy. He had just told me he was a spy, but he seemed to me little more than a college boy.

"I thought spies weren't supposed to tell anyone they were spies."

"I wanted you to know."

He was tall and thin and had grumbled all night about the inadequacy of the single bed. He was a sprawler who slept on his stomach, which prevented us from curling efficiently together on our same sides as I had always done with Buster.

My room was on the rue des Beaux Arts, a third-floor walk-up, rudimentary and charmless, except for the long window that opened up to a little balcony and, over rooftops and chimney pots, to a view of the Seine.

"It seems like it could be dangerous for you to tell everyone

9

you go to bed with. I could be a spy for the other side—if there is another side."

Now I was lying on my stomach, head on my folded arms, looking at him intently. He was on his back, looking at the ceiling. He turned his head to face me so that we almost touched noses. He smiled. "You're not smart enough to be a spy."

"I know," I responded, completely agreeing. "It's amazing when you think what a genius my father is." Masefield had read Daddy's books. Muir Scott was his name. A famous philosopher.

"What about your mother?"

"She's an athlete like me." Since our noses were almost touching, I stuck out my tongue and he touched the tip of it with his. We both had the kind of tongues you could fold up the sides of into a U shape, only he could do a double fold, a pleat! He said he had only shown this trick to three people in his life and that I should feel honored. I did.

"Being an athlete doesn't preclude being intelligent," he said.

"It does with me and Mom. Did I tell you I was a sailing champion?"

"Yes."

"I repeat myself a lot."

"I like repetition. It enriches the facts. There are always new nuances. Anyhow"—he harked back to a former remark of mine, which he often did as though he thought old things over while he went on talking about new things—"I don't go to bed with a lot of people. Hardly anyone."

"My mom and I," I went on, ignoring his harking back so I could keep on talking about sailing, "both have twenty-ten vision so we can see the wind shifts on the water before the other sailors in a race, or perhaps by a leaf dropping a couple of miles away, or smoke rising. We can spot a hole, which is no wind. So we get to choose the favored side of the course with more information and accuracy, before the others."

"Before the other side, if there is another side," he echoed. "Yaeger has that kind of vision—the flier who broke the sound barrier. He could see enemy fighter planes before they saw him. This was before radar."

"Ted Williams, the ball player, has it. He can see what kind of pitch is on the way to him. He can see the spin of the ball."

Masefield looked back up at the ceiling dubiously, frowning and sticking out his lower lip. Not very spylike, I thought, to so readily show his disbelief.

"Poor Daddy has Coke-bottle glasses," I said. "He looks so frail and vulnerable because of the thick glasses, but he actually is very strong. He has big shoulders and arms, which I inherited. For a woman I have amazing upper-body strength."

"I noticed," said Masefield. He turned to look at me again. His eyes were violet with black lashes. His hair was black and curly, and his skin really white. "You brag a lot for a woman, too. Even for a man."

"I know, but it's not because I'm insecure, it's because I really think I'm great. Do you want to arm wrestle?"

It was while we were arm wrestling, bodies all atremble from the strain of it, sweat standing out on both our brows, one jaw clenched, I forget whose, that the phone rang. It would be a long time before we would wrestle again and learn who was the strongest.

"Your mother has run away," Daddy said.

We talked for about twenty minutes from Paris to Inverness, California. Meanwhile, Masefield, alleged spy, got up and dressed. He had the longest back I'd ever seen, slightly curved, like a scimitar. Even as I was listening to all this astounding news from Daddy ("Your mother has run away. I have gone away with Chris"), I was thinking how Masefield's back would give him trouble later in life and that I loved him and wanted to keep him, especially as I might never find another man who loved repetition. It was as if I had to think about something other than what Daddy was saying, something in the far future, because I was practically in shock.

Masefield went out and returned with coffee and croissants. By then I had said good-bye to Daddy and was just standing there—a sailing champion in Paris turned to stone.

If Masefield hadn't come back, I'd probably still be standing there, but he asked me something and I clicked back into the present and started talking. Only it made no sense.

I have a problem writing, I write backward and upside down and mix my letters, and that's how I addressed Masefield, as if I were reading aloud my writing at the worst of times, gibbering and making expansive gestures as if the gestures would make sense of the words.

The remarkable thing was that as I was doing this, I had a memory of talking to Andy that way, being a baby and talking to my brother in this language that only he and I could understand. Andy, whom I had no memory of at all, who had died when I was small, along with the language and my memory of him. To suddenly recall this scared me and made me gibber more.

Masefield calmly sipped coffee and munched pastry, waiting until he could be heard to say, "Please start from the beginning. I can't make any sense of it."

His wonderful calmness brought me to my senses. He's right, I thought. I have started at the end and am talking backward. "I don't know where the beginning is," I said in English. "I can't make sense of it either."

"We'll find a beginning and make some sense. Sit down"—he gestured to the bed, as he had the only chair—"have some cold coffee, and tell me the background facts about your town and family and childhood."

Scrunching some pillows behind me, propped so I could see him as I spoke, I told him about my family, beginning with my brother, Andy, who died when he was five and I was three. My folks lived in Berkeley then, Dad teaching at Cal. Then they moved to Inverness and there was just the three of us: Mom, Daddy, and me, Sunny. And Chris made four—my best friend, who was often staying at our house because her father drank and beat her.

Our house was on a hill above the bay, but you could walk down a quarter-mile path to our boathouse and pier where Mom and I kept our boats.

Mom never got to sail as much as she wanted to because she

was at Daddy's beck and call. He depended on her for everything. The business of running the house and his professional
life was the main thing, but as well he was like a child, so
unable to do for himself was he. She fixed every one of his
meals, poured his drinks, answered his phone, received his visi-
tors. I often wondered if she didn't bathe and dress him. No, I
never wondered at any of it, her devotion was such a known and
accepted fact of life. He even liked her to just be there in the
room while he was reading or writing, and of course he never
left the house without her.

I guess my friend Chris always had a crush on him; he was
handsome and had a boyish charm. He could be surprisingly
silly and fun to be with for one with such a big throbbing heavy-
duty brain.

Now that I think about it, Chris gradually began doing things
for him too.

Mom was never silly. I can't remember hearing her laugh.
She took her life with Daddy very seriously. She was the great
man's caretaker and protector. Also she never stopped mourning
Andy. I could tell she was happy out on the water, but still, she
never laughed.

"She looks like me," I told Masefield, getting back to the
present tense because after all, just because Mom and Daddy
weren't together anymore didn't mean they weren't still alive.
"At a distance we could be sisters. Straight, shiny, white-blond
hair, pale blue eyes, big white teeth, tanned skin—except I'm
stronger. I could always handle the sails better in a storm while
she'd capsize. Still, she's a better sailor, much better. She taught
me all I know, but I think she kept some things back.

"For all that Mom and I are so much alike, I am closer to
Daddy. I think that her consuming love for him, and maybe still
for Andy, prevents her from loving me. But Daddy has always
been affectionate. He would play with me."

It took about half an hour to say it all to Masefield and for
him to delete the repetitions and get it sorted out. "So those are
the background facts," I finished, "or were the facts. Now everything has changed. Everything!"

"Wait." He held up a hand. "Don't tell me about the phone

call yet. Let's go out to a cafe for some breakfast and you can tell me there. I'm so hungry my stomach thinks my throat is cut." He passed me my clothes. "While you're dressing, give me a quick sketch of Inverness so I can get the picture."

I said it consisted of little more than a post office, market, gas station, gift shop, an inn, a bar and restaurant, a yacht club—a woodsy peninsula of land with the Pacific Ocean on one side and Tomales Bay on the other, one point of a big triangle that is Point Reyes. The bay, thirteen miles long, was probably caused by an earthquake, as the San Andreas Fault goes right down the middle of it.

"The mouth of Tomales Bay is the breeding ground for great white sharks, but I've only seen a couple in my lifetime. Point Reyes, aside from some ranches and a lighthouse, is a wilderness area renowned for being the windiest point of land in America. We get a lot of fog as well as wind, so the bad weather plus the shaky ground keeps Inverness the one-horse town that it is, pop- ulated by retired people, living-off-the-landers, artists, and writers—in short, people who don't need to go to work, San Francisco being fifty miles of curving roads away, people who want to be left alone."

Dressed: I in white skirt, blue blouse, and sandals, Masefield in khakis and polo shirt, we went out to a cafe for me to tell what Daddy said, first calling the airline to arrange a flight back and wiring my friend Buster that I was coming home.

Walking to the cafe, hand in hand with Masefield, I remem- bered the morning I left home. The instructions from Daddy about my graduation present were to go to Paris and only to Paris. I'd been a country girl all of my life and now, said he, it was time to learn to be in a city and I might as well begin with the greatest city in the world. It was time to get civilized, to see the originals of the paintings I'd only seen in books, to use the language I'd studied but rarely spoken, to deal with thousands of people each day instead of three or four, to not sail.

He was the world-famous philosopher, translated into four- teen languages. If the intellectuals of the world paid attention to him, I might as well too, lowly sailor though I was, without two thoughts to rub together.

My last morning in Inverness, I was up before Daddy for once, sitting at the kitchen table, a cumbersome oak one with lion's paws carved in the ends of the legs, having a bowl of granola heaped with fruit. I heard the squeak of his huaraches as he walked slowly down the stairs. He never hastened.

He was fifty-three years old, about five feet ten, big shoulders and arms, getting soft in the middle. If he hadn't been an intellectual, he'd have had a body like a strong man. He wore, as usual, baggy shorts and a cotton shirt. He never wore a sweater. I don't think he owned a sweater. Sometimes he would put on a windbreaker or, with pants, a tweed jacket. None of my family feels the cold much. He had red hair going gray, a mustache, thick rimless glasses in front of distant brown eyes.

He went up to the barometer and tapped it for a proper reading, grunting softly to himself. He looked out the window to corroborate his findings (fog), then turned to me and smiled. "Sunny," he said.

"Daddy," I replied.

Having established who we were, he joined me with a huge china cup, more like a bowl, of tea. This was the one thing he could make for himself. He could boil water really well. "You're going away today," he said.

"Yes."

You wouldn't think a great philosopher would make such self-evident statements, but that's the way he talked and it was actually very pleasing.

"To Paris," he said.

"Paris, France. Your idea. I'm going to get civilized."

"High time."

"I'm going get lonely too," I reminded him again, for I'd already mentioned this a time or two. "Horribly lonely. You're sending me into exile."

"No, Sunny, I'm not. This is exile, not Paris. We are so isolated here on this last lonely sentinel of land." He looked off as if he were quoting—probably from something he'd written himself.

"No sailing! How can I live without sailing? Is there any water at all around Paris that I can at least look at? And I'm going to miss you so much."

"Humph, I notice you mention the sailing first."

"I'm already dying from the loneliness to come."

"No, you are not," he said sternly. "You are not going to be lonely in the least and I'll tell you why." He smiled. "You are going to have a friend in Paris. His name"—he paused as if inventing it—"will be Masefield."

It was three weeks before Masefield showed up at my pension, which was good because by then I was not only civilized but, to my way of thinking, a woman of the world, independent as all get-out. I knew Paris like the back of my hand and spoke French like a native, or so I imagined, and I had a gang of friends from all nations. I didn't even *need* this promised Masefield, which was again good, because then I could just fall in love with him because he was so great.

He stood at the door of my room, looked me over rather gravely, and said, "My father is a friend of your father's. He asked me to look you up—paid me to, actually."

"How much?"

Masefield, violet eyes coolly shining from a dramatic gaunt white face, said, "A lot. But from now on"—he smiled slightly —"I'll do it for nothing."

We spent the next two weeks together, but it wasn't until the last night that we slept together and he told me he was a spy.

Of course we didn't know it was the last night, so it was pure luck that we spent it that way. We'd been going along as if we had all the time in the world, little knowing we were coming into the final hours. I was standing in front of the mirror, brushing my hair, when Masefield came up behind me, put his arms around me, and let me feel the fine swelling of himself on my rump. What a great feeling. Responding instantly, although completely surprised, I turned to meet it and him front on and to embrace him in return, standing on tiptoes so as to be nipple to nipple, sex to sex.

He bent his scimitar shape to mine.

With shaking fingers we unbuttoned buttons, removed each other's clothes, and, in lockstep, I the one walking backward, crossed the floor to the bed, Masefield entering me as he lowered me down onto it, both of us still shaking like leaves until overwhelmed by the larger quakes from within that minimized the surface sensations. We flung our bodies about like little baby birds trying to fly but falling back into the nest each time, several times almost falling out of it.

It seemed like we made love all night long, but we must have slept or Masefield couldn't have grumbled so about the single bed. When either of us awoke, we woke the other one. It got to be that we longed to sleep, to please please be let alone even as we were initiating yet another connection. We must have made full orgasmic love six or seven times that epic night, and to think that on top of all that we tried to arm wrestle. Good thing the phone rang or it might have been the end of us—complete cardiac arrests of two so young, for neither one of us was about to give an inch on this vital question of who was the strongest.

# 2. WANTING A SMOKE

$S$unny and I walked hand in hand to the cafe. I was exhausted. She may or may not be stronger than me, but she definitely had more endurance. I was dying for a smoke. A nicotine hit would give me a lift. But Sunny was hanging on to my hand for dear life. It was like I was leading a blind person down the street, deaf too. She'd really been knocked for a loop. That gibberish she'd gone into was the weirdest thing, bar none, that I ever heard in my life.

For some strange reason she seemed ten times more interesting to me now. Sure I'd fallen for her the moment I set eyes on her, but, face it, we had nothing in common. She couldn't appreciate any of my finer touches like carrying *The Castle* around in my coat pocket with just the K showing. She hadn't even known who Kafka was, let alone read him. As for Beckett...

Hard to believe she was Muir Scott's daughter, a fact that certainly enhanced her possibilities at first but didn't matter now because she was, primarily, Sunny, one in a million.

Possibly I could light a smoke with one hand, but I never had before and I'd hate to fumble it. I'd have to practice for the future.

Whenever I discover there's something I can't do with insouciance, I practice until I can. It had never occurred to me that I would need this particular art since I'd never held a girl's hand walking down the street before. I probably never would again, but who knows, I could lose an arm. There was a better chance of that than a repeat of this. Of course a cigarette lighter would simplify the matter tremendously, but there's something devilishly attractive about these little French matchboxes containing tiny waxy matches. Lighters are prosaic. Lighters are Rotarian.

The ideal thing would be to stop being so contemptibly self-conscious as if every eye were on me every time I made a move and every eye were assessing the move. But that will take years. And meanwhile, the idea is to get good at the moves.

I squeezed her hand and she sent me a grateful look with those washed-out blue eyes of hers that wouldn't even look blue if they didn't have the world's whitest whites around them. Those eye-whites didn't know the meaning of the word blood-shot.

After last night and this morning, I felt completely bonded to the woman. I felt like she was my wife!

Which was the one thing I couldn't plan on having in this highly planned life of mine. There wouldn't be time or room.

But, over and above the lovemaking, it was the news about her father and mother and friend that made me see her as a vulnerable, complicated person instead of the simple sailor girl. Because I've always loved mysteries. I've always loved finding out. And now I felt like a window had opened showing a whole landscape of Sunny heretofore unspied and unsuspected.

I mean, anyone who talks a whole other language that she didn't even know she talked until today . . . !

And imagine her loving her family so much! Anathema to me, who hardly knew my parents to say hello to, having been sent away to school since I was six and raised by a nanny until then.

However, I could understand her feelings re: best friend, Chris, who had not only absconded with father Muir, but deserted Sunny as well. Doubly betrayed!

The trouble was, I was about to be the world's biggest rat by not going back to Inverness with her to help her get to the root of it all.

I was working now in Paris, then I had ten days off before going behind the Iron Curtain, which my work here was setting up.

I could take that ten days by joining Sunny in California, but I really didn't want to. I wanted to go to Spain.

What I had to do was cut her loose just when I realized I loved her—or maybe *because* I realized I loved her.

But first I had to put the spotlight of my brain on her problem and be all the help that I could be.

We got a good table at Aux Deux Magots. Everyone turned to look at us as we sat down. I knew we were a knockout couple. Sunny didn't notice or care. She was unself-conscious about herself and uninterested in anyone but whom she was with. We could leave this place after an hour and she wouldn't have noticed one person. Whereas I could tell her what every single person there looked like as well as what he had for breakfast— and if he liked it.

She didn't really notice buildings, either, didn't see the sights. She was a terrible traveler. She once said, and really believed it, too, "There's much more to see on the water than on the land."

"Well," said I, "I suppose so, if you count all the waves."

"No, no, not the waves. It's everything else!"

"Oh."

We sat down and I looked around avidly. Maybe I'd see Hemingway.

# 3. SEEING HEMINGWAY

We went to the Aux Deux Magots cafe because Masefield admired Hemingway and always hoped to see him at one of his haunts. Before the disruptive phone call we had talked of going to Spain to look for him at the bullfights. Daddy had said I was to go no farther than Paris. Masefield said parents' rules and injunctions were made to be broken. This had never occurred to me.

"Will you still go to Spain?" I asked as we sat down, the realization now dawning that Masefield and I would be parting and that this was unbearable. I couldn't bear to think that his life would go on without me.

Masefield lit up one of those vile-smelling Gauloises and said through the smoke, "Yes."

We gave the waiter our order. It was a balmy soft blue day, wisps of clouds. "Is that being a good spy to go and watch bullfights?"

"Spies are supposed to watch everything: bullfights, operas, and wars."

Two nights ago, Masefield had taken me to L'Opéra, *Samson and Delilah*. He loved the stuff. I learned that I didn't. I was not a cultured person. It's hard to be a cultured champion—there isn't time. But now there was time, or had been, could have been, if I didn't have to go home.

The waiter brought me coffee and Masefield a Pernod.

"In Spain I will get to drink absinthe instead of this cheap imitation," he said. "It's available only in Spain and Lichtenstein. It rots the brain," he added with some satisfaction.

"I just don't get why you're a spy," I said sulkily. "There isn't even a war going on anywhere." I seemed to be trying to make him feel useless. I felt somehow jealous of his spying as if it were another woman.

"There are invasions. Russia is going to invade Hungary. Tell me about the phone call from your father."

I did. Masefield, hunched over his Pernod, listened carefully and asked questions. Every so often he would straighten his back, raise his head, and look around—for Hemingway, I guess.

I began, "They've both run away. Mom and Daddy. Mom first. It seems that just before Daddy was to have run away with my friend Chris, which he has now done, my mother herself ran away."

"I don't understand." Masefield looked so utterly puzzled that again I thought that if he was a spy, he should learn to mask his reactions a bit. "Does a grown man run away?" he wondered aloud. "It doesn't seem very civilized."

"He could hardly stay in the same tiny town where Mom still lived! Not to mention Chris's father, the scum of the earth! He's mainly running from her father, Barthold, who's a horrible brute and who must be madder than a billy goat at Daddy taking up with his daughter.

"I'm pretty mad myself, but I'm just so unaccustomed to thinking of Daddy ever being in the wrong that what he has done must be right. They must really love each other. Still, he's . . ." I stopped to figure. "Thirty-five years older than Chris! And poor Mom!"

"I don't get why *she* ran away."

"It could be that she ran away because she learned of his upcoming desertion and figured that by running away herself she'd throw a monkey wrench into his plans because he'd have to stay and look for her."

"Why? I should think her going off would fit in perfectly with his plans. He wouldn't even have to feel bad about leaving her if she had already left herself."

"Because she hasn't actually left. She's gone looking for Andy. . . ." My voice quavered. I cleared it. "Which is like she's gone crazy."

"Andy is your little brother who died."

"Big brother, he would have been. It turns out that all down through the years Mom would periodically go looking for Andy. She'd sail out in the bay and just stay out there for days. In a small boat, mind you, without a cabin. There'd be no way to catch her and bring her in, even with a powerboat. If they spied her—"

"She spied them first," Masefield interjected, "because of her incredible vision. She can see the spin of the sun."

"Yes, and then she'd hide. There are a bunch of little coves and thickety inlets. I never even *knew* any of this until today! She got better as the years wore on, but even then Daddy had to keep her always by his side so she wouldn't go looking for Andy. So all these years when I thought she was protecting him, he was actually taking care of her. Can you believe that!"

"I don't know. Should I? Should you?"

"Of course I should. Why would Daddy lie?" I retorted, feeling insulted for Daddy—or maybe for me for believing him if he had lied.

"I thought they were in Berkeley when Andy died."

"Yes, but in those days they'd weekend in Inverness and it was while there one weekend that they lost him and they never found his body. Then Mom refused to leave Inverness and Daddy had to stop teaching and stay there with her. I only just learned all this today!" I paused to get a grip on myself and pondered, "Maybe that's what he meant by saying Inverness was exile." I told Masefield about my conversation with Daddy on the day I left, the last lonely sentinel and all that. "Isn't it weird? And to think I never knew all this until now."

Masefield smiled and I realized it was at my repetition. There certainly was nothing in the content to smile about that I could see.

And yet it's true that telling it to Masefield seemed to settle the waters and clear them. Telling it the second time, at least, for the first time I'd only gibbered and got scared remembering Andy, having that quick glimpse, like a shutter opening, into my childhood, my babyhood, seeing how close I'd been to him, how dependent. And then he drowned. Mustn't that have been awful for me too, as well as Mom? And what about Daddy?

Anyhow, Masefield, by getting me to tell about everyone running away, was helping me to cope and to know what to do, was making the dizzying information manageable.

The waiter brought me a cheese omelet. I thought I would just pick at it, but in fact I was ravenous. I wished I'd ordered two.

"And Chris and Daddy fell in love just after I left." Even as I said this it sounded unconvincing. I'd only been gone a month and a week. Something must have begun with them before then. Mightn't I even have been *sent* away as part of the plan? Maybe Daddy didn't want to get me civilized so much as just plain out of the way.

Painful thought. Masefield's fault to have sown seeds of distrust, and why heed him—he, who didn't know Daddy one bit? Why? Because of our night of love, that's why. That one night seemed to have bound me so close to him that a lifetime of adoring Daddy no longer had power.

Had Chris and Daddy had such a similar night that all his years with Mom were rendered insignificant?

"Of course there's no way they could stay in that tiny community with Mom right there. Poor Mom. Now she's gone batty and this time Daddy won't look for her because he thinks she's done it purposely, emotional blackmail, to keep him there—so I have to go home and find her and take care of her. He says he wants his chance at happiness. Do you think that's right for a philosopher?"

"To want to be happy? No, I guess a philosopher should know better."

"No, not that, Masefield, to foresake his responsibility."

"Maybe your mom will take responsibility for herself, now."

"Maybe she will. Daddy said not to come home, to leave her be, but I can't. It's too sad, and too embarrassing."

"There's Hemingway," Masefield said. He directed his glance to a man passing by. He was a fine-looking man, and except for the fact that his face was tired and sad, he looked like Hemingway. He looked like Hemingway, only not bigger than life, just human-sized. Not so human you'd ever expect to see him in a laundromat or a grocery, but not like King Arthur, either. If it even was Hemingway. It probably was. From the look on Masefield's face, it must have been. I thought it would be a sad letdown for Masefield to see his hero was so tired-looking, but it wasn't. I suppose even King Arthur looked tired sometimes. I know Daddy did.

I guess I expected Masefield to jump up and chase after him, but he didn't move a muscle. "Don't you want to say something to him?"

"No. There is nothing to say. It is enough to have seen him. There are certain things and places and people one has to see in a lifetime. I have a list. I see Paris but I don't have to say anything to Paris. There is nothing that Paris doesn't already know."

"What other people must you see?"

"Your father, for one."

"Is that why you loved me, so you could meet my father?"

Masefield didn't answer. I was ashamed. It was a childish thing to say. It was petty and shabby. But what if it were true? It could be true. But then his father wouldn't have to have paid him to look me up, would he?

"I'm sorry. It's happened before that people used me to meet my father. That's another reason Daddy's in hiding now. He just published a book that's got this big cult following going and people are seeking him out in greater multitudes. He's a shy man, actually."

"That's three reasons he's given you to allow himself to run away and hide." Masefield put up fingers as he recounted the reasons. "Your mother. Chris's father. The multitudes. Too bad. I wish he had just given one reason. It makes you wonder if the three aren't camouflaging a fourth one that's the real reason."

Again a hot retort in defense of Daddy came to my lips, but again I saw what Masefield meant, again felt disturbed and baffled.

"Masefield, I wish you'd come back with me. You could help and I know I'm going to miss you terribly."

"I'm sorry. I can't come now. But I will come when I can."

"I love you," I said. "You don't have to say you love me too." I waited for him to say he did love me. After all, he'd shown me his tongue trick that he'd only shown two other people.

Instead he said, "I can't say so since I'm unable to back it up with being able to be with you and help you. I'm in no position to love you. I will come, I promise, but I won't ask you to wait for me."

"I will wait for you."

"Don't, Sunny. Go on with your life."

"But you said you'd come."

"I will."

"Then I'll go on with my life but I'll wait, too. Masefield, can I see your list?"

"It's in my head and we have more important things to do and talk about our last day in Paris. Right now we're going to see the catacombs. We are going to walk through miles of skulls and bones, through the dank underground of Paris, carrying a candle, and then we will come out into the beautiful sunlight, sit by the river Seine, and eat strawberries."

We looked for our waiter. Then we saw Hemingway again. He came over to our table.

# 4. MUIR SCOTT'S DAUGHTER

Passing Aux Deux Magots, wondering whether to stop for a *fine*, I noticed a beautiful young couple of Americans, talking intently. They were sitting at an outside table so I passed close by them.

From the corner of my eye, I saw that they recognized me. That's how it is now. I can't go back to the good old cafes and be anonymous. I have to burrow deeper into the arrondissement.

Walking on, growing less self-conscious, I was able to turn over the image of the two young people in my mind's eye and I realized I knew the girl. Or, I was pretty certain I did. She was Muir Scott's daughter.

I hadn't thought about Muir Scott for years and now, as I did, I felt good. It was a lightening of the heart to think of Muir Scott because he was one of the best, one of the big boys. It seemed to me that if I went back to the cafe and talked to Muir Scott's daughter, I would feel even better. And a drink would make me feel good, too.

They were astonished when I came over to their table. The boy was on his feet in an instant. "Mr. Hemingway!" he said.

No one had called me that in a long time. It had a good sound.

He introduced themselves to me as Masefield and Sunny.

The girl was as fresh and fair as a milkmaid except that her blue eyes had the ancient mystical look that sailors and pilots (some ocean sailors and some bush pilots) get from looking farther than most people for longer times and maybe from having to think a lot about winds. No one else has to think about winds so much as pilots and sailors.

I remembered that her mother had these same eyes. I began to think that it was the eyes that made me recognize her because wasn't Paris full these days of healthy blond American girls like this one?

And the boy had a singular look about him that was at once strange and familiar. It gave me a chill to realize that the familiar was that I was reminded of myself at his age when I was that slim, that fervent, that smart. I knew this boy was going to be in for a lot of trouble in his life and it made me like him right away. At the same time I felt suspicious, realizing that I was not alone in this feeling, that a lot of people would like this boy right away, and the reason was because he had charm—not as in charming and delightful, attractive and pleasing, but charm as in magical power, captivating and enslaving—something I didn't have as a young man and don't now as a man a lot less young, although I can think of one or two people in my life who did.

She told me yes, she was Muir Scott's daughter, so I sat down.

"But I don't remember ever meeting you," she said. "How could you know me?"

"It was a few years ago. You didn't actually meet me. I was talking to your father and you breezed through the room on the way to go sailing. You stopped and told your father your plans and what he was to tell your mom, and I thought: To her, he is nothing more than a father. She has no idea."

"I guess I still don't," she said.

"And I thought: He is not even going to introduce me to his daughter because it isn't important to him that I'm Ernest Hemingway and therefore he doesn't think it would matter to her and that's the way he is."

"But was he glad you'd come to visit?" she said, and it was

sweet because I could tell she was afraid I felt hurt by her father not thinking I was important. She hadn't understood what I meant.

I could see that Masefield understood and that it pained him a little that Sunny didn't.

"Glad? No. That would not be the word. Your father is too wise to feel such things. Let me just say that he was completely there for me."

"I'd hate to be so wise I never felt glad." She laughed.

"I'd read his A *Question of Being* and he is a man who fully embodies what he writes about. He knows how to be. I myself," I assured her, "was glad as hell to meet him."

Masefield smiled.

"How is he?" I asked her. Instead of responding, she began to look miserable, slumping down in her chair and picking up her fork as if there were still an omelet on her plate.

"He's run away," Masefield said, and I looked at him to see if he was being ironic, but he wasn't and it seemed to me extraordinary and enviable that Muir Scott had run away. I felt jealous. I wished I had thought of it first. It was a simple and fine thing to do. But there was nowhere for me to run to and I couldn't be alone anymore. That was one thing I didn't know how to be anymore—if I'd ever known it.

After I felt jealous, I felt sad, feeling I'd lost him. I couldn't go see him again if he'd run away. Even though I wasn't going to go to see him it was nice to think I could if I wanted to and that he'd be there if I came, being not glad to see me, just nodding when I showed up at the door, and saying, "Ernest," giving me to feel I had just been baptized.

Done feeling jealous and sad, it began to seem funny to me, his having run away.

"It's not funny," she said.

"I'm sorry," I said, laughing. "Is your mother all right?"

Masefield said, "She ran away, too," and Sunny glared at him and then it was his turn to look abashed and say he was sorry. "Actually," he explained, "she *sailed* away. Not far. She's right there on Tomales Bay. Now Sunny has to go home and get her... uh, to come ashore."

"Please don't say anything more about it," Sunny asked in a strained voice, and Masefield complied, falling silent.

"You'll find her," I told her, and she looked at me gratefully, deciding, I guess, that in that case she herself would tell me more about it.

She told me about her mom looking for Andy, and it was marvelous.

Long after I left the young couple I still had the wraithlike image in my mind of her mother, sailing the long slender silver bay, day after day, her mystical blue eyes sweeping the waters over and over for the body of her small son who had drowned some fifteen years before.

# 5. BUSTER

After Masefield and I had gone through the horrible catacombs, which was worth doing if only to appreciate how lucky we were to live on the earth not under it or, in my case, which is even better, on water, and to be alive not dead, we returned to my pension to make love seven more times but instead fell asleep—not individually and grumblingly, but tight and close in each other's arms and legs.

We got up in time to have dinner before getting my night flight.

At the airport, Masefield said, "I'll tell you one thing about my list. You'll be the first person on it that I'll have to see again in my life, that once wasn't enough."

This wasn't exactly saying he loved me, but it was close. Then I did a double take. "Wait a minute. How come I was on your list to begin with?"

Masefield looked like if he was a blusher, he would be blushing, but you can't be a blushing spy. Bad enough to make all the giveaway faces he did.

"I saw a picture of you once," he said.

"You told me your father had paid you to look me up," I accused him.

"I lied. It's terribly important to me not to seem eager when I see these people and places on my list."

"Will you seem eager when we meet again?"

"Probably not. By then I will have mastered noneagerness. It still needs work. Did you notice how I leapt to my feet for Mr. Hemingway, almost knocking over my chair? Bad action."

"About this next meeting of ours, Masefield, will it be soon?"

"I can't say, Sunny."

"I'll be waiting."

I flew off at midnight feeling desperately desperately sad, leaving my lover so as to go back to the home from which my only three loved ones, Mom, Daddy, and Chris, had just run away.

I was forgetting Buster. I did have one loved one left at home and his name was Buster. He met me at the airport. He was standing there with a big smile when I came out of customs. He was carrying both our motorcycle helmets. "Hi, champ!" He hugged me in his gigantic arms. His embrace was a home in itself.

"Oh, Buster, thanks so much for coming."

"Are you kidding? Of course I'd come." We walked to the garage, me taking the helmets, Buster carrying my duffelbag. He asked me about my trip, although I could tell he was bursting with something to say, which he soon did.

"I've got a new bike," he said happily. "The Norton Manx."

"Named after the Isle of Man race," I remembered. "And the cat."

"Right. It's a five-hundred-CC single-cylinder engine, which means it has an internal displacement of one-half liter."

"Which means?"

"That if you turned the engine until the piston was at Top Dead Center and you poured fluid into the cylinder as you move the piston down and you fill the cylinder with the piston at Bottom Dead Center, the internal displacement of the cylinder would be the amount of fluid that it took to fill the cylinder."

As we walked, he explained this to me carefully, intently searching my face to see if I understood what he was telling me.

I was able to form the facial expression he sought even though I didn't understand engines at all, being a wind girl myself. I always tried to please Buster, if not by learning, at least by *looking* as if I were learning.

But with Masefield, I had hung on every word he said about anything, stretching my mind to its limit so as to follow his words and train of thought.

Buster's elegant machine stood among the cars like a unicorn in a field of cows.

Buster kissed me. "I'm so happy that you're home and that I got the Manx in time to meet you with it."

He tied my duffelbag on and I sat behind him with my arms around his waist, my head laid wearily on his block of a back. I'd been traveling for over a day and this would be a two-hour ride. I was glad the method of travel didn't allow me to talk, as I would have to tell him right away about Masefield.

Buster and i had been together for a year or so, friends, and lovers, too, the only one before Masefield. He was one of those guys who was too sweet to live and he probably wasn't going to live long, either, if he kept up his motorcycle racing. He was now twenty and had been Northern California Junior Champion at age seventeen. Of course he always told me I was going to be the one to go first, sailing being much more dangerous, which wasn't a bit true. It's just that he was afraid of the water! One time he tried to come out on the boat with me, but it was pure misery all the way. Luckily I wasn't afraid of the road or we'd be in big trouble about seeing each other. I loved to get on the back of his bike and let the miles roll under.

Buster worked on an oyster farm across Tomales Bay from Inverness. I'd originally met him sophomore year in high school, same class, he being a couple of years behind himself. He was an orphan who'd been raised as a foster child by a woman everyone called Mama Clausen, in Petaluma, the nearest big town to Inverness, the egg capital of the world, as it's called, and also famous for its arm wrestling world championships, held every fall in the local tavern.

"Okay if we take the mountain road?" he asked after we'd crossed the Golden Gate Bridge.

"Sure."

We took the winding road over Mt. Tamalpais and I let myself go with the rhythm of the road and the dance of his machine, having complete confidence in Buster. If one day he destroyed himself on the thing, it wasn't going to happen with me on the back of it. He wasn't a wild man, he was a pro. It's all a matter of being present, Buster would say, and I knew what he meant from my sailing. I guess that's what Hemingway meant about Daddy being wholly there for him. But that was different because Daddy was never in any danger—at least not that I knew about. Maybe if you are a philosopher of renown, you are in constant danger of doing or saying the wrong thing.

Buster was even less cultured than I was. He was the kind of man who always had grease under his fingernails from tinkering with his machine. He didn't finish high school. At least I did that. He could read but he didn't, which Daddy always said was just as bad as if he couldn't. He and Mom didn't approve of Buster for me one tiny bit.

But what a sweetheart. What a lover, of everything and everyone. He had more friends than God. I loved Buster. I always would. But I wasn't *in* love with him. I always knew, and always told him, that the day would come when I would fall in love with someone, and now I had. God knows I wanted to be in love with Buster, but I couldn't force myself, could I?

I hadn't even thought about him once the whole time I was gone.

We walked into my big empty house, which was designed by a famous architect: a series of big rooms on different levels with floor-to-ceiling widows looking out at woods, bay, and hills, with beige rugs and furniture—the color of the hills this time of year. It was not a cozy house, I realized for the first time, and definitely too beige, but maybe that was just because no one was there to greet me.

Daddy would have kissed me and danced me rather sedately around the room. After dinner, we would talk way into the night. Mom would have greeted me in an abstracted way as if wondering where she'd first met me—but would have a special dinner all planned, the table beautifully set, flowers in my bedroom.

Buster was looking at me with concern, always so sensitive to my moods. After Masefield's gaunt face, chiseled features, fascinating expressions, Buster's face looked like a cow's, a big cow's face, all eyes and broad planes. His chin was as big as most people's heads. He had a brute body. Both my legs could fit in one of his.

"Are you tired, Sunny? Do you want me to leave you and come back later?"

"No, please don't go. It's so empty."

"Okay," he said happily. "I made an oyster stew. Let's have supper. It's only four o'clock, but who cares." He bustled out to the kitchen. Of the two of us, he was the domestic one, loved to cook and clean.

I was pretty quiet during supper. Buster chattered away about a motorcycle trip he'd taken to Mt. Lassen. When he brought in a carrot cake, we started to talk about what had happened to my family. Buster said, "I'm sorry. It's really awful. It must be like your world has turned upside down."

"Did you talk with Chris before she left?"

"Yes. She's pregnant."

"By Daddy!"

"Bart would have killed her if he found out. She was having morning sickness and was very scared. They had to get away, fast."

A fourth reason, Masefield, I thought, holding up his fourth finger in my mind: Mom, Bart, the multitudes, the baby.

"Golly," I said sadly, "Chris and I were always going to be pregnant at the same time and raise our kids together."

"I know," Buster said feelingly.

"Now look." I gazed sadly out the window. "How far along was she, Buster? How long have she and Daddy been together? Why didn't she tell me?"

Buster shrugged. "How could she?"

"How could she have done it, Buster? I just don't understand."

"I don't know, Sunny, I don't think you decide to fall in love; you just do."

This was my opening. I seized it before I chickened out. "Buster, I fell in love in Paris."

His eyes widened and sort of locked into place. His jaw dropped.

I told him the whole thing, talking fast, words falling over themselves, how I'd met Masefield through Daddy and the two weeks we spent together. "I couldn't help it, Buster. I didn't want to. It just happened."

"It's okay." Buster held up his hands. "It's okay. We'll forget about it."

"No we won't. I can't. I love him. His name is Masefield." Now I was starting to repeat myself as usual. "I'm really in love with him. He's coming here. I'm going to wait for him."

Buster just looked at me with his big eyes as if they were his ears, as if looking at me would hear the words and make sense of them. But he was also talking, saying, "No. No. No." Every time I said something, he said, "No."

"Not no. Yes. Yes, Buster, truly. I'm sorry, but it's so."

"Did he . . . did you . . . you didn't . . ."

"Yes we did!" I said, almost shouting now because it wasn't fair for him to look so hurt. I'd always told him it would happen someday. He knew I wasn't *in* love with him.

He made a moan that sounded like his insides had split open. He put both hands up in front of his face and a whole bunch of tears burst out between his fingers.

"Oh, Buster, stop. Please don't. Please!"

Pushing away the plates, he lowered his head onto his arms and sobbed.

Part of me wanted to go to him as I had always done when he was hurt or sad, but how can you be the pain giver and the comforter too? And the other part of me hated him for carrying on so and for letting someone like me hurt him so bad. Anyhow, Buster and I weren't at all the crying types. Champions don't cry. He was letting us both down by acting like this, by being a baby.

"Stop it!" I shouted. "Buster, cut it out!"

I'd gone over to him and was hitting him. I was just standing there punching him on the head and shoulders, flailing away and crying too. Yeah, I started to cry too. He just kept his head bowed and took it.

When I realized what I was doing, I stopped and ran out on the deck, closing the sliding door behind me so he'd know not to follow.

That's the kind of person I am, I thought bitterly. When my best friend starts to cry, I beat up on him.

After a while, I heard his motorcycle start up, the Manx that he was so happy about. He'd been so happy about it and about me coming home. Putting the two together.

Now I had nobody.

Except Mom, I remembered. I looked out at the darkling bay, at the towering hills of grass on the other side containing the rosy light of sunset. Somewhere, out there on the bay, was Mom, and I was going to find her.

A turkey buzzard floated past on a current of air, wings and tail spread but not flapping. A beautiful sight, my kind of sight. Nothing like that in Paris. Those birds knew something about winds.

I went to my room, took off my clothes, crawled into bed, feeling bone weary. All over the walls were sailing pictures and pictures of Buster racing, his bike leaning so that his shoulder was practically on the track. I had sailing trophies on my shelves. There were plain white curtains on the window and my wallpaper was little blue forget-me-nots. My bed was covered with a puffy sky-blue comforter and lots of white pillows. I had white cotton sheets. On the oak floor was a woven rug, white with green oak leaves in a random pattern. It was a nice room. It was a child's room and it didn't have anything to do with me anymore.

I wound and set my clock and luckily fell asleep before I could think about anyone, especially Buster, because deep down I knew that losing him was the worst loss of all.

# 6. WANTING TO DIE

The pain was so bad I wanted to die. I got on my bike meaning to ride it to the end of the point and sail over the cliff into the sea experiencing in one move the two things I most dreaded: being in water and dying.

But I couldn't carry out the impulse because it went against every cell of my being to destroy a beautiful new machine. Even if it washed ashore, the saltwater would have wrecked it.

All these thoughts were running through my head, each one crazier than the next. At the same time there was a clanging in my brain like someone was banging on sheet metal. I looked around to see if anyone was.

It felt like my blood had turned around and was running the wrong way, tearing my body apart. My heart was killing me. It hurt so bad it seemed like it had to be an attack and I should be lying on the ground instead of getting onto my bike. My bike. My great new bike. God, I'd been so happy a few hours ago, going to get Sunny on the thing. Sunny coming home and me going to get her!

I loved her so much! I loved her so much!

I'd hear about people killing themselves and I could never understand it. Life was so wonderful. There were so many things to do, and to try to do. So much stuff to think about. And you want to find out what's going to happen with everyone. And love! Sunny!

But now I know that people kill themselves to stop the pain, the pain of the moment, the clanging, and the awful emptiness of looking at all the hours days years to come if you are still going to be alive and Sunny doesn't love you.

Loves someone else!

Masefield. What kind of name was that? What was he, some Frenchman? How could she say she loved him after only two weeks? Two weeks was nothing. A drop in the bucket. We'd been together over a year and knew each other inside out. And what did she mean she was going to wait for him? Wait for him to do what? Why wasn't he here if she loved him so much? Why didn't he come back with her or why didn't she stay? What kind of a man would make love to Sunny and then not stay with her for the rest of his life? I guess the kind of guy who named himself Masefield would, or, if someone else named him it, who didn't get rid of the name as soon as he was grown up.

Well, heck, I should be glad he isn't here. It isn't as black as it seems. I'm here and he isn't. How long can you keep loving someone you never see and who you only knew for two weeks? How long do you wait? Did she say when he was coming? Did she say tomorrow or the next day? It sounded pretty vague to me.

But do you keep hanging around someone who doesn't love you, who loves another guy, named Masefield, who she's hugged and kissed and . . . Oh, God, don't think about it.

Do you hang around eating your heart out wishing she'd love you again? No, never, only a fool would do that. Even if she did love me a little, it wouldn't be the same. There'd always be the specter of this Frenchman. I'll go away instead. I'll go far, far away, or over the cliff, one or the other, tonight.

Instead I went to Mama Clausen's and threw myself into her arms, pressing my face into her chest just like I did when I was a little kid.

When I walked into her house I had this weird feeling that it shouldn't still be there. If my solid relationship with Sunny had altered so suddenly and completely, why hadn't everything else changed, too? Why wasn't it a different century?

But there Mama was: big, fat, unflappable. I told her what Sunny had said and all that I was feeling because of it.

She held me fast in her arms, calm as a tree, heard me out, sat me down, made me tea, and told me to go right on back to Sunny.

She talked to me in her accent that nobody had ever figured out what in heck language it came from. Mama never told one person about her past. She always said that's why she took in little kids that had no past, because she never had one, either.

"Buster, when you came to me all that long time ago, you never spoke a word for two damn years and now you talk your head off at the drop of a hat. It's good, though. It helps to be able to speak of things that tear you up. It gives you ease. I like to think I didn't just teach you to talk but to talk *a lot!*"

She laughed and I knew she was going to tell my talking story, which she did. "I remember the first time you spoke aloud. Your voice was all cracked from disuse, like a rusty hinge. It was something you needed to say so bad that it was worth the risk of opening up, of trying out those dried-out, stiffened-up vocal chords. There was so much feeling in you fighting to bust out."

She'd told me this story about my first words a hundred times. Probably the reason I fell in love with Sunny was that she repeated herself as much as Mama Clausen.

She looked at me all soulful. "You said, 'Mama, I've got an idea.'"

Here she always laughed because she built the story up to sound like it was going to be something emotional I said, like "I love you, Mama Clausen," but instead I'd gotten this idea how she could have room for more children by building loft beds with ladders and I was so excited about it, I didn't want to just draw a picture, I wanted to speak. I wanted to communicate.

"Never mind that now, Mama Clausen," I begged her. "I need your help. I'm dying. I'm about to stop speaking again for another two years."

So she talked to me about Sunny. She explained to me that

monstrous things were happening to Sunny with her family and that I had to stand by her no matter what. She was losing everyone she loved: her mother, father, friend, now me. Also she had lost her Paris lover, though maybe she didn't realize it yet.

I must not think about myself and my own feelings, she said. Love was standing by the person in their time of need, which she knew I knew but the pain was making me forget. Pain was a big part of love, she told me, but you couldn't let it drive you away from the person. "Love isn't just bluebirds," she finished, "it's snakes."

I nodded, head bowed, as though I'd been handed a penance.

I stayed with her a couple more hours, doing some stuff for her around the house. The hot-water heater was acting funny. One of the burners on the gas stove didn't light. The fireplace chimney needed cleaning.

Doing the work made me feel better physically. My head had stopped clanging and my blood had settled down, but I was still having the heart attack and every time I thought of Sunny and how she loved this guy, this Frenchman or whatever he was, my heart would go blammo like some string broke and the sweat would come pouring out of my whole body, cold and clammy like the seawater I dreaded.

I stood at the kitchen sink, stripped to the waist, washing off the soot from the chimney. "All your problems are with fire, you know that, Mama, with keeping the flame going and keeping things hot?"

"It means my own flame's getting low, Buster boy."

"You're not that old yet, Mama. You're not even a hundred."

"I feel like I'm two hundred and ten."

"No, that's just your weight."

We laughed. Then one of her little foster kids woke up with a nightmare and Mama sent me to talk to her. I sat on her cot, held her hand, and told her all about how I'd come to Mama Clausen when I was a scared little kid who'd lost his folks if he ever had any to begin with, too scared even to speak. "And now I'm hardly scared of anything.

"Or I wasn't until today when the scariest thing of all happened to me—I lost my girlfriend." The kid was dropping off to sleep, but I kept talking. "She stopped loving me today and the world dropped right out from under my feet. I guess that's why I didn't need to ride over the cliff. I'd already gone over it. I still feel like I'm out there, hanging in space, nothing to hold on to, feeling dizzy and disoriented, some clanging sound all around me or in me."

I stopped and peered at the kid. This wasn't a very nice bedtime story. But it was okay, she was asleep. So I went on.

"But Mama said Sunny needs me and she does. She's lost everyone else. Even this crumb, Masefield, let her down and didn't come back with her. And then I start acting like an idiot and leave her all alone her first night home when she said the house was so empty."

Suddenly I felt an urgency to get back. What was I doing mumbling over this sleeping kid with poor Sunny all by herself in that huge house?

Sunny needs me. Mama said so. But it had taken all these hours for that to sink in.

I raced downstairs, grabbed my jacket, and, waving good-bye to Mama, leapt out the door and onto my bike. "I'm coming, Sunny, I'm coming!" The Manx responded like magic, carrying me over the countryside like a wish being fulfilled.

I didn't know when this guy was coming, but I made a vow I would stick around helping Sunny until he did and then I would simply go, head out of town without any fuss. Because loving someone is wanting that person to be happy even if you're not included.

I felt the tears come like they had when Sunny told me, but I knew I was just feeling sorry for myself now.

And I knew that the pain was going to get better, but it wasn't going to go away. I was never going to feel again the particular happiness I had known with Sunny. It was going to be different. I was going to have to learn to live with the snakes.

I stopped at my cottage to get my sleeping bag and toothbrush. It did me good to see the place, which was about the size of a ship's cabin, with my few belongings all neatly stowed. It gave me a feeling of comfort to see that I did belong somewhere, had a place that was mine with my things in it, and that I wasn't hanging in space after all. It steadied me a lot.

Then I jumped on the Manx and went the ten minutes farther to Sunny's house, coasting down the driveway and letting myself in as quietly as I could so I wouldn't wake her.

# 7. ABANDONED HOUSE

I heard Buster's motorcycle in the distance and woke up. It was one A.M. I heard him enter the house. We never locked up. I felt frightened. Because I'd woken so suddenly from a heavy sleep and bewildering dreams, I couldn't think straight and felt afraid Buster might have gone crazy with grief and come back to kill me.

I sat up in bed and looked stupidly around for something to protect myself with. There was nothing but white pillows that had tumbled to the floor. I reached for two of them, toward what end I don't know.

By then Buster was at the door of my room. I turned on the bedside lamp. He looked overwrought but not crazy. His hair was disheveled, and in the shadow of the doorway it made him look like he had pointy ears and horns. I pictured him riding his bike all over Point Reyes without his helmet, being a wild man not a pro.

He said, "Sunny, I'm sorry I acted like that and went away without a word."

How like Buster to apologize for my meanness.

He came and sat down at the end of the bed. I released the pillows I was holding against my chest and stomach to shield me from his pain. "I know you didn't mean to hurt me, Sunny. You couldn't help it that you fell in love with the guy."

"Oh, Buster..."

"Wait a minute. Let me speak. I've been thinking about it for hours. I want to stay with you."

"No..."

"Not for me, for you. Now's a hard time for you and I don't want you all alone in this big house. I'll sleep in the living room. You need somebody. You haven't anybody."

"Buster, you've got to find a girl who can love you like I do Masefield and you can't do that staying here with me."

"I don't want anyone but you. I never have and I never will."

"Don't say that. That's why you can't stay with me because you'll keep hoping."

"It's not hoping. It's a fact of life. If I don't stay, I'll worry about you the whole time and probably have to set up camp outside your door to keep an eye on you. I'll just stay until you're through this trouble, 'til you find your mom or until the guy comes. We're friends, aren't we? That's what friends are for. When he comes, I'll go away. I'll leave the state."

"Buster, I just don't know what to say."

"We'll talk some more in the morning. I'm going to sleep now—in the living room. I've got my sleeping bag."

He left and I heard him settling down. I couldn't get back to sleep. After a while I crept to the living room to peek at Buster. He was in his sleeping bag on the floor. Not even on the couch. He was a big mound with his lumpy face sticking out, the moonlight shining on it in its path across the floor. He was already asleep, looking like he'd been hit with a sledgehammer.

It was so unnatural for him to be there on the floor and me alone in my bed. We'd always been so glad of the times we could find to sleep together, not to make love so much as to just be together, mostly Buster doing the talking because he loved to tell stories. He could make stories of any tiny little thing that happened. He had the gift of gab. I loved to fall asleep to Buster's stories. But there he was, alone in his bag in the moonlight with no one to talk to.

I went back to my room, to bed, and to sleep.

I awoke at dawn, remembering a conversation that I'd had with Chris one day back in the spring when we were out on the bay in my boat, planning our lives. "We'll get pregnant together," Chris said.

We were becalmed and just lying back and talking drowsily, both on the leeward side, sails hanging in the shape to catch a breeze if one came. Water and sky were bright blue, and the hills were so green it seared your eyes to look at them. The light was dazzling, not the sunlight, just the light light—which was different on Tomales Bay from anywhere else, as if God had turned it up a couple of notches. Maybe it was because of all the water and the bare hills for the sun to reflect off. Or something to do with all the light-colored cows. Or maybe it was just that the landscape, being in fog so much, seemed doubly illuminated when it wasn't.

"You of course will be carrying Buster's baby," said Chris, "although after the first three months I don't know how it will fit in your stomach. Come to think of it, I don't know how his cock does."

I giggled. "It doesn't go into my stomach."

"I bet it does."

"I don't know whose baby I'll carry," Chris said. "I don't care, either, as long as he's just like your father in every detail. Whenever I sleep with someone, which is often, I pretend—"

"If Andy had lived, you could have married him."

Chris had some Indian blood and her hair was so thick and long that when she washed it, it took a day to dry. She was drying it as we talked. It hung down, enclosing her. She lit a cigarette and I watched the smoke come up off it because it would detect a breeze before the limp telltale at the top of the mast.

"Our babies will grow up and be best buddies like we are," Chris said. "We won't let any man take us away from each other."

"Right," I said. We'd had this conversation a dozen times. It was a good conversation.

"Buster we can count on."

"But I can't marry Buster. I'm not in love with him. I suppose I should stop seeing him, but it would be just like not seeing you because I can't marry you. You shouldn't stop seeing people you love just because you can't marry them."

"That's what I think too," she said.

Oh, Chris, I thought woefully. Why didn't you tell me on that day when we were floating around so long that you loved my dad? Maybe you didn't know then that you loved him; maybe you knew but never dreamed anything would come of it. But how did you even find time to be together without Mom around? She never left his side.

But Mom found out. And that's why she took off, hoping to keep Daddy here looking for her. She must have heard Daddy and Chris talking about leaving.

But how do we *know* that was the reason she left? We're just presuming.

Buster said when Masefield comes, he'll leave the state. What if Mom left just so Chris and Daddy could be together? Out of love for Daddy, she left.

No. Buster might do that but not Mom. And anyhow, she didn't leave; she went crazy. She was right here on the bay being a loony bird.

I rolled over in bed. From the living room I could hear Buster lightly snoring, still deep in his sledgehammer sleep. I got up, put on a robe, walked to the living room, and squatted by Buster's head. He opened his eyes and smiled. "Hi, Sunny."

"Buster, when Masefield comes, don't go. There's no reason we can't all be friends. And if we can't, it will be for me and Masefield to go, as long as I've found Mom by then. How could I stand to think I drove you from your home?"

He looked pained again. His face scrinched together, grew smaller. He closed his eyes. But that was all the more reason for me to speak of Masefield, so he wouldn't begin to pretend it wasn't true.

He talked with his eyes closed. "It isn't home here without you, Sunny," he said. "That's why I went off to Lassen when you left for Paris. The sun stopped shining. The birds stopped singing. It was awful."

He sat up and opened his arms to me. Without thinking, I snuggled into them, wrapping mine around his waist. It was so natural. "Let me make love to you, champ," he murmured. "Please. Please. It will be like it was before. I know it will. Oh, God, Sunny, please."

I wrenched myself away and scrambled to my feet. "No, Buster, it won't. It can't be. Because I know what love is now. When I parted from Masefield in Paris, I wanted to die. When I left you here in Inverness, I didn't feel anything. Nothing! And I didn't even think about you the whole time."

Buster just sat there with his head hanging down. If he started to cry again, I'd kill him.

"This is why you shouldn't stay here," I said sternly. It was true. He was just letting himself in for a lot of misery.

I turned and went into the kitchen to make coffee. In a few minutes, Buster came in as if nothing had happened, nothing had been said, and started making a pancake batter. He sliced in bananas and threw in some chopped walnuts. "If I don't stay, you won't ever eat," he said nicely. "You'll just drink coffee."

I realized how like my dad I was. Buster, Mom, or Chris always cooked for me. It wasn't that I didn't want to; it was that they did want to. It wasn't that I ever asked them to because I'm happy just nibbling on uncooked stuff, but they all seemed to think I'd starve if they didn't. But I wouldn't. When I'm hungry I eat. I sleep when I'm tired. And in between times, I sail.

Maybe it was true of Daddy, too. He let people take care of him because they wanted to and he just went along doing what he did. He'd just be, like Hemingway said. Mr. Hemingway, as Masefield called him. How startled he'd looked at someone not calling him Papa.

After breakfast I took a tour of the house to try to get a sense of what had happened. Again I was struck by how cold and impersonal it looked. Mom and Daddy's bedroom also looked forlorn of personality. Maybe it was because their own powerful personalities filled the place so much that I never noticed the house was so blah. They just let the architect's own vision and design stand, without cluttering it up.

Then I realized that Mom always had bunches and bunches

of flowers all around the house, which put the endless beigeness in its place, in the background, and provided the color and beauty and spirit.

They were her own flowers, and everyone was always so amazed at the garden she grew in this climate.

I went out to the garden, wondering if she'd arranged for its care in her absence, but I soon saw that one doesn't make arrangements for going crazy as one does for going on a trip.

It was very dry. The earth had cracked in places. Some weeds had already come. The flowers hung their heads in dismay. "Buster!" I called. It was more like a wail.

He came running out. "Aw, gee," he said. "What a shame. Dad's wonderful garden. I'll give it some water." He went to turn on the hose.

"No, it was Mom's garden, Buster. She was always out here working." Buster had rarely come to the house since he was so disapproved of here, still . . . "Why'd you think it was Daddy's?"

He looked confused. "I thought it was your dad's." He started spraying the garden with great sweeps of his arm. "He understands flowers so well, and loves them so much."

Buster was obviously as confused as he looked. I decided not to pursue it. Sometimes Buster wasn't quite all there and I didn't like to push him. I resumed my tour. The situation was really coming home to me now. In Daddy's study I got my second shock, a much bigger one. Three of the walls were filled with bookshelves and they were practically empty! About three-quarters of the books were gone.

This was a monumental moving task. It showed me that Daddy had really gone for good. What's more, he must have accomplished this after Mom had gone looking for Andy, which seemed so callous, so unlike Daddy. Somehow I'd imagined him making his getaway in the dark of night, out a window, down a knotted sheet, Chris waiting with the motor running. But no. It was a calculated, premeditated move with boxes and boxes of books.

The couch and easy chair that were set before the fireplace looked abandoned, the pillows all puffed, no impression of anyone's body. There were no flowers, no vases of dying flowers, the water all green. Who had emptied all the vases and washed them? Chris?

Not Daddy, who I never saw wash a thing in his life. Too busy being.

I returned to the garden, dragging my feet. What I needed now was to get out on the water. Everything would make sense to me there.

"I'm going off sailing for the day, Buster, to see if Mom's anywhere out there. Dad said she took her boat to go looking for Andy. Did we talk about that?"

I couldn't think what I'd told Masefield and what I'd talked about with Buster.

"Andy? Who's Andy?" Buster looked all amazed. He was still waving the hose around, a thumb on the nozzle to make it spray. Now the hose hung down, the water splurting out, making a mud puddle by his feet.

"Andy, my brother who died when I was three. They think he drowned in the bay."

"I've never *heard* about him." Buster looked at me like I was crazy, like I'd gone around the bend and invented a brother. "You never talked about him once."

"Well, I . . . I . . ." It was true, I never had. And Mom and Dad never talked about him, either. There were no pictures. I'd talked to Chris about him because I'd known her when I was little, when it seemed important and impressive to have a dead brother, so I'd told her then, when I was five or six, and had sometimes mentioned him over the years, like that time in the boat when she was drying her hair.

Another reason was that Buster and I talked about boats and bikes and what we did that day, but we never got into any deep stuff, never thought of having any deep stuff to get into.

Now I tried to talk about Andy to Buster, saying, "I was only three when he died. I don't remember him at all, and my folks never talked about him to keep the memory alive. Except I always knew that Mom loved him best and that she still grieved. In fact, I don't think Mom ever loved me—maybe Daddy didn't, either—because of losing Andy. Maybe they blamed me for not being the one to die instead."

These are things I'd told Masefield, a stranger, that I never told Buster. I told him now, as if to make it fair, as if the telling, not the lovemaking, had been the real disloyalty. Also, it seemed easier to say the second time, now that I'd tried it out. Or the third time, rather, since I'd gibbered it at first. The gibbering had unlocked things for me somehow.

"Then Daddy told me on the phone that every so often Mom goes over the edge and goes looking for Andy on the bay, just takes the boat and goes out there and stays for days, comes home half-dead with hunger and exposure. This has been going on for years. He'd go looking for her, but she'd be impossible to find. Eventually she'd come home on her own."

Buster shook himself as if he were shivering. Probably he was feeling cold from the water getting all over his legs. I went and turned the hose off.

"How long has Mom been gone?" I asked him.

Buster counted back. "Probably about a week."

"I wonder how she eats and where she sleeps. I suppose I should drive around to the different coastal towns to see if anyone's seen her."

"Why don't I do that? I'll take the day off."

"Would you, Buster? That would be a great help. Just think, maybe by tonight we'll have found her!"

# 8. GONE, GONE

I rolled out of bed, hit the floor on my back, and lay there looking at the ceiling where some asshole spider was trying to haul a fly into his net.

Another bad morning. Another stinking day. If I could make it to the shower, maybe I'd find some life in me to go on with. My body felt like it had fallen out of a truck and got run over by a Caterpiller tractor. I'd've liked to crawl. Why walk? Give me one reason. No one to show off for except me, and I didn't care. When there's no one around, you just don't care no more. No fucking dignity left.

Still, I walked. What the hell. I walked, kicking crap aside as I went. Chris only gone a week and the place looking like a shithouse. The bitch did more work around here than I realized.

"The bitch, the bitch," I moaned, turning on the water and walking in under it. Ice cold. "Gone. Left without a word, not one. After eighteen years. Gone, gone."

I turned on the hot and soaped myself, then the cold again, then off. But there was still water coming from my eyes. Self-pity. Sorry for myself. No fucking dignity left. Eighteen years.

I put the kettle on the burner and threw in the coffee when it boiled. Managed to find a clean work shirt and my jeans. Heard Carl drive up in his pickup. Second later, in he came.

"Hey, buddy, are you ready?"

"Let me drink my coffee."

I lit a cigarette. Tremble in my hands. Used to be rock steady. Strong horseman's hands trembling like an old woman's.

"This place is a mess, man. Chris still away?"

"She's gone for good."

"I still can't believe that beautiful kid going away with an old guy like that."

"The bastard, the bastard."

"Hell, it wouldn't be so bad if he weren't married, even being that old. He's rich as Croesus and smart as hell and I never heard anything but that he was a real nice guy."

"He's evil. He poisoned her against me, her own father."

It's true, I thought but didn't say aloud. She came to despise me, always comparing me to him. She looked at me with contempt where there used to be love. And it weren't just from me hitting her. I always hit her but we always made up afterward and she knew it was for her good that I did it. She always looked up to me until he got so important. I was her daddy. I was the handsomest man she ever saw. I could ride a horse like the very devil. She'd come to the rodeos and cheer me on, all lit up with pride. We'd go rodeoing across the country and she was my little lucky piece. I was the calf-roping king until my body got so broke up from the falls from the broncs over all the years of biting the dust.

"Come on, Bart. We got to be going. But one other thing, man, in case you haven't heard . . ."

"Tell it."

"They say she's carrying his kid."

I almost blacked out. The blood drained from my body and rushed back in again like that tidal wave that came back into the bay after the quake. I could feel my eyes bulge from the rush of it. "I'll kill him. I'll kill the sonofabitch if he ever shows his face around here again. I don't care how the hell fucking famous he is. I got a right to. The law's on my side."

"And that's not all. They say the wife has disappeared."

"She has, eh? I guess I know something about that. I guess I can put two and two together about that."

"What do you mean?"

"Never mind. I know what's what. I used to go over there, just to check out the place, just to see what the hell was goin' on there with my kid. I've seen some things. That man isn't the Jesus fucking Christ philosopher he makes out to be. I'll kill him. I'll go after him. . . . "

"Good luck. No one knows where he is, not even his own daughter, who's come back from Europe to look for her mom."

"Oh, yeah? Whereat is she lookin' for her?"

"On the bay. She thinks her mom's out sailing around on the bay because that's what her daddy told her."

"Her mom's sailing the bay all right. Only she's sailing around *under* it, sailing around on the bottom mud, round and round, scooping out a hole to make a grave for herself, that's where, if you want to call that sailing."

# 9. CALL FROM DADDY

We didn't find Mom that day or even that week, although once I saw, way in the distance, a boat like Mom's, which was a one-design, and a person in it with white straight hair like mine.

Others—sailors, rowers, fishers—thought they sometimes saw her too. Pretty quickly everyone in town knew I was looking for her. When they approached me about it, it was embarrassing for them as well as for me, so no one would quite look me in the eye as they said things like "I think I saw your mother the other day between Hog Island and Pelican Point," because whoever heard of such a thing as a woman, a mother, who took off in a boat and lived a phantom existence on water avoiding everyone, even her own daughter. Still, there were enough of these vague sightings that, put together with my own, I felt sure she was out there.

Of course, she could see them before they saw her, and her boat was very fast, and she was a fabulous sailor. But my eyes were as good as hers, my sailing adequate, my boat fleet and trusty, and I knew Tomales Bay every bit as well as she did. A couple of times I tried to take binoculars along, but it was impossible to keep them steady enough to see through while on the water. They would just make me feel more frustrated.

The summer was passing. How would she live when winter came? How did she live now? What was the point of it all?

Daddy called toward the end of my first week back, his second week away. It wasn't a good connection. He sounded far away and probably in a phone booth. Daddy and I both tended to shout over long distance anyway. Still, we managed to have a good talk.

I was in the kitchen, having a cup of herb tea before bed. The only rooms I used were the kitchen and my bedroom. I was beginning to hate the whole house. Buster didn't like it much, either. He spent most of the time he was here in the garden, and we both liked to take our meals out there.

He still slept in his bag on the living room floor.

"Mom has been spotted a couple of times in the far distance," I said to Daddy after our greeting.

"Yes, that's always how it was. Vague sightings. I'd be out on the bay by the hour with my little outboard and I'd see her, but when I went after her, she wouldn't be there anymore until I began to think I really hadn't seen her in the first place, that my sightings were mirages under the sun or wraithlike forms in the fog, false images from a fevered imagination."

"What was the longest she ever was out?"

"A week, once. Yes, a week."

"But Daddy, it's been two weeks now!"

"She must have made camp somewhere. She must be going to some other town for supplies. Your mother is very resourceful."

"Even when she's batty?"

"Don't say batty."

"What should I say?"

"It's a psychic break. Periodically she suffers a psychic break and she imagines it's the day we lost Andy. She relives that whole week of our losing Andy."

"Daddy, what was Andy like?"

It was as if the long distance, his distance, allowed him to speak out about Andy at last.

Or maybe it was simply because I finally asked him.

"He was the most wonderful little boy." There was a gruffness to his voice I'd never heard before. "He was so brave and spunky and strong and smart. He was unbelievably smart. At five years old, he was reading my books."

"Are you kidding?"

"No."

"Is that why you never talked about him to me, because he was so much . . . so much . . ." My voice faded. "More wonderful?" After Andy, I must have seemed like the world's biggest letdown. I was ten years old before I could read decently, and now, at eighteen, on bad days, I still could labor over the directions on a box of Bisquick.

"We never talked about him because it was so painful. I guess we taught you never to talk about him for the same reason. Your mother was so fragile. Any mention of him could set her off on her mad hunt."

"Daddy, how's Chris? Is it true you're going to have a baby?"

"Yes. She's fine. We're both fine and happy."

"Can I speak to her?" I had a funny feeling like he was holding her hostage and I should be able to hear her voice for proof she was there and alive and okay.

"She's not here right now."

The feeling heightened. "Where is she?"

"I'm calling from a phone booth."

"Didn't you want her to know you were calling me?"

"I didn't tell her about your mother. I didn't want to upset her in her delicate state. It's hard enough that she had to leave Inverness and you. She thinks I told your mother I was leaving with her, but I didn't. I was going to, of course, but she went looking for Andy before I could."

Suddenly he changed the subject. "Sunny, how did you like Masefield?"

My heart pounded to hear someone else say Masefield's name. "I loved him," I said.

"Did you, Sunny? That's wonderful! He's a fine boy. A Rhodes scholar, you know."

"He didn't tell me that." Daddy had been a Rhodes scholar.

Obviously Andy, had he lived, would have been, too, since you have to be an extraordinary athlete as well as a brilliant student —the all-round incredible person. If you're one of the thirty or so selected each year, you get to go study at Oxford. All my feelings of inferiority surged to the surface and as well I felt hurt for Buster. I could tell Daddy was thinking: At last she found a boyfriend I can be proud of.

So, instead of feeling happy that Daddy was pleased, which part of me really was, I got contrary and said, "I just meant it was fun to fool around Paris with him. You were right about Paris. It's a great city. I wish I could talk about it with you."

Realizing I couldn't, my voice cracked. "Daddy? I miss you. I miss you so much. When are you coming home?"

I was forgetting about the books, the empty shelves. I was forgetting about the pregnancy, Bart, Mom, the multitudes. But what about me? Didn't I matter at all?

"Time will tell," he said. One of his favorite expressions. For a philosopher, he was very vague. He didn't seem to have any real system of thought that I could see—but who was I to say since I, at eighteen, hadn't read his books like Andy did *at the age of five?*

"Daddy, where are you and Chris?"

"I can't say, Sunny."

"Please tell me."

"I'm sorry. I'll call again soon. I love you very much. Goodbye."

I waited for the click and even after it I kept the receiver to my ear, seeing him in my mind's eye, hanging up the phone, pushing open the accordion door of the booth, stepping out onto what street? In what town? I pictured him sighing—Daddy was given to deep sighs—then lifting his chin and looking about, maybe for Chris. He would be wearing his Panama hat, baggy but perfectly tailored pants, a spotless cotton shirt.

I replaced the receiver and had to laugh a little when I realized that, I, too, had sighed deeply and audibly.

Right. I laughed a little, but I felt sadder than before. It seemed so unfair that I was left holding the bag and that nobody seemed to care.

Well, I had taken it upon myself. Daddy had said not to come home from Paris.

I wondered if Mom knew I was home. Had she seen me looking for her? If so, was she sane enough to know it was me, or, in her mind, was I only three? Maybe she was only out there because she thought I was in Paris and she didn't need to worry about me worrying.

I decided to write to Masefield. I'd been putting it off, not because there weren't millions of things to say but because I have so much trouble writing. I can't spell at all. I reverse my letters without even knowing it. Sometimes I can put the right letters in a word but they'll be in the wrong places. Mostly I put letters down that never belonged to the word since the beginning of time. Chris used to wonder how I even thought of them in connection with the word. She'd always correct papers for me before I handed them in at school. She did admire the fact that my bad spelling never hindered me and that I went right on and wrote whatever came to mind undaunted. I could express myself.

I must say I felt damned daunted and hindered writing to Masefield, however, knowing I had no one to correct for me—I could hardly ask Buster—but once I got going, the pen flew over the paper and I wrote so much it ended up more like a package than a letter. I told him all about Buster, Mom, Dad, Chris, everything. I even told him all about Barthold Blainey, Chris's father, and what he'd said—the miserable sonofabitch.

It was one evening when I was in Point Reyes Station, the little town where Buster lived, about five miles from Inverness, at the land end of the bay. Bart came out of the saloon. I'd like to say he came reeling out, but he was one of those stiff-legged drunks who instead of getting loose, get wooden. I don't know what he looked like because whenever I looked at him I just saw red, which was probably accurate—the color of his face from all the booze-broken blood vessels.

Although, since he was an Indian, maybe his face was brown as ever. He'd been a good-looking man at one time.

I just prepared to pass on by. I hadn't spoken to the man for years because of the way he treated Chris. I hated his very guts. I used to dress her wounds from the blows he'd give her. She'd never go to the doctor, never would report him to the police. He tried to abuse her sexually, too.

He was respected by the men around because he was a good ranch hand.

"Hello, slut," he said, which is what he always called me and Chris, a good example of his charming personality.

I walked on, looking straight ahead, but he grabbed hold of my arm. "Can't find your old lady, can you. You're looking in the wrong place, that's why. She's at the bottom of the bay, not the top, because that's where your daddy put her." He sneered out the word Daddy. "Chris thinks he's so fine, so perfect. Wait'll she finds out he's a cold-blooded murderer."

"Take your stinking hands off me."

He didn't. He held on tighter. "You tell your old man that if he ever shows his face around here, I'm going to blow it off him. You'll have to go looking for it in the next county."

"The man is pure slime," I told Masefield in the letter. "I tried to kick him in the balls, but he blocked me and pushed me away so that I was left sprawling in the street while he coolly turned and walked away. I got up and was going to go after him to throw him down and jump on his head, but then Buster arrived and held me back."

I stopped writing for a minute, remembering the moment Buster grabbed hold of me and kept me from going after Bart.

"He accused my daddy of murder, Buster. He said he murdered Mom!"

"There's talk going around," Buster said. "I was hoping you wouldn't hear."

"Talk! Talk! It's Bart and his foul vile diarrhea mouth, the drunken bastard. I'll kill him for starting that rumor. I'll kill him. It's all because of him Daddy and Chris went away. They'd be here if it wasn't for him. I've got to find Mom, Buster, and when I do he's going to make a public apology. Oh, Buster," I said despairingly, "where is she? Why can't I find her?"

"She's out there," Buster said. "You'll find her. You've already seen her."

I redoubled my efforts. Mom wasn't the only one living a phantom existence on the bay; I was too.

The days went by and I began to lose it. I felt drained and discouraged. Instead of being alert out there, I'd fall asleep at the tiller. It was lucky I didn't have accidents. On rough days I'd come home cold and drenched. I never use to feel the cold and wet, but now I did. Buster would bundle me up in warm dry clothes and make a hot dinner. "You'll find her," he promised me for the fiftieth time. "We know she's out there. Today Ned Hatcher thought he saw her out between Blake's Landing and Nick's Point. That could place her campsite up Walker's Creek somewhere. I'll go look tomorrow. It's only a matter of time. Hang in there, champ!"

I wrote all of this information to Masefield, bundled it into a manila envelope, and left it on the table to mail in the morning. Buster would see it when he came in, but that was good. I wasn't talking about Masefield much anymore—what was there to say?—but I didn't want Buster to think I was forgetting him and get his hopes up. I wanted Buster to understand that I was still waiting for him.

Three weeks later, I got a letter back.

# 10. LETTER FROM MASEFIELD

I finished up my day at the oyster farm, another cold foggy summer day. The weather had been horrible all month, but now it was near the end of August and in September the fog usually lifted and we'd have a couple of warm clear months before the winter rains set in.

End of August and still no Mom.

People were shaking their heads over poor Sunny.

Those of them, that is, who weren't tilting their heads, looking off sideways, and reckoning the woman was dead as a doornail.

"Come on," I'd say. "Sunny's seen her. Plenty of folks have seen her. What kind of father would set his daughter to looking for a woman who wasn't there?"

And then they'd look farther off than sideways and reckon that the murdering kind would.

Which is just what my boss said as I was about to leave. I answered, "That's crummy talk, and you know where it originated. From Bart, who doesn't have his daughter to beat up on anymore. We're talking about Muir Scott here, one of the gentlest men who ever walked."

"Nice of you to say that since it's my understanding that he never thought much of you."

Probably for the same reason Bart hates Muir, I thought, but didn't say. A gentle man will dislike his daughter's lover and a violent man will want to kill him.

"Why in heck should he?" I asked, and meant it too. A high school dropout, knockabout motorcycle racer isn't a father's idea of a dream son-in-law—at least it wouldn't be mine.

I walked to my cabin to change before going over to Sunny's, stopping at the Point Reyes Station market to pick up some food for dinner, something it never occurred to Sunny to do. She'd be dead of malnutrition by now if it weren't for me.

At the market, too, people wanted to talk about Sunny and her mom. It was beginning to gripe me. It'd be one thing if they really cared, but they were mostly just curious and gossipy.

At home I showered, then lay down and fell asleep. I woke up ten minutes later completely refreshed and in a better mood, feeling more forgiving toward the citizens of the two towns. It's only human nature.

I lay thinking about the garden. I was having so much fun with it. I'd been taking some of the different ferns from the woods and creating a fern garden in the shady part. I was thinking it would be nice to put a little pool in there, a sort of stream, and how it would be a simple matter to fashion a pump to keep the water running. It would be a fountain, really, but so embedded in the earth and rocks it would look natural. And then, wouldn't it be something to go to Mount Tamalpais and find that rare orchid that grew there, the calypso, and get some of those for the garden, just a few, not to in any way deplete the mountain's small store of them. I bet I could learn how to propagate them. They were tiny, no bigger than my fingernail, bright pink. Those, along with the white violets that grow everywhere around here. And moss. And baby tears . . .

I got up and dressed because I knew it was possible to lie there thinking about the garden and its possibilities and have hours go by. Jeans, red plaid shirt, leather jacket, and I was set to go. I hung my damp towel out on the line, where it would get damper probably, stuffed the shopping into the saddlebag, and took off for Sunny's.

When I got there, I saw a letter from Masefield on the kitchen table. It had been opened. I knew she meant me to see it. I don't know if she also meant me to read it, but I did. I put down my bag of stuff, picked up the letter, kicked the chair free of the table, and sat down to read, not even calling out to see if Sunny was home. It was pretty long.

"Dear Sunny," he wrote, and without fooling around with any tenderness, he got right to the heart of the matter.

"Mightn't these sightings of your mother that the townspeople speak of actually be sightings of you?"

This was something that had not occurred to me. I guess it took somebody far away to see what was plain and what made awfully good sense.

But his not being here also prevented him from getting the sense that she *was* out there, a feeling so strong you could touch it. You just knew she was, that crazy as it sounds, it was true.

"Someone not emotionally involved should question Bart Blainey and find out if his suspicions are based on any kind of fact or whether it's all just rage. The man should be officially questioned. It's the best way to stop the rumors."

That we can't do, I thought. If we started an official investigation, it would be admitting we thought there was foul play and it would be nothing but trouble and grief. As long as we believe she's alive . . . well, then, she is alive.

"I know you are thinking that the best way to stop rumors is to find her. In any case, your father can't be charged when there is no corpse, so don't worry. It would be splendid if you could produce a witness who saw her after your father left and *before* you arrived.

"I am in Torremolinos, Spain, which is on the southern coast, about eighty miles from Gibraltar. It is the most unbelievably beautiful little fishing village. From the sunny beach there is a view of the snow-covered Sierra Nevada range. The place is completely unspoiled. I think it must be like Inverness. Except for El Remo, a fancy hotel down the road, there are only two cafes, the morning cafe called Manolo's and the one for the rest of the day and night, called The Bar Central. Here the few expatriates gather each day: artists, writers, retired English colonels, the odd Swede in search of sun, or an Australian on a world odyssey. But the town is mostly Spaniards, shouting their staccato Andalusian across the square, where their donkeys drink from the fountain.

"Until yesterday anyhow. Yesterday the donkeys scattered when a huge thing drove into the square that was neither auto- mobile nor trailer but both, a sort of live-in van which had been made especially in Germany. The inside, all in wood, is exactly like the captain's cabin of a ship. It belongs to Count Von Luckner—another of the great men on my list (the second great sailor). Known as the Sea Devil, he captured American ships during WWI from a windjammer! He would sail up to the ships as friendly as could be, looking like a romantic old clipper ship, and suddenly would reveal herself as an auxiliary cruiser armed to the teeth. Guns would appear. He'd take our officers aboard as prisoners and wine them and dine them. Never killed a soul. He tramped across America as a youth and knew Buffalo Bill. He's in his late seventies now but still a big powerful man who radiates life and joy of life. I could go on and on about him, but I want to tell you about the bullfights in Málaga. I saw Dominguin."

I skimmed over the bullfight scenes, wondering when the heck he was going to start telling Sunny how he loved her and missed her and was coming to see her.

But instead he returned to the subject of the count, who as a young man had learned magic from an Indian fakir, which, said Masefield, as far as he could tell, was really crowd hypnosis, and which he would love to get the count to teach him how to do.

"For instance," wrote Masefield, "the count asked for some- body's ring. Then he took a little potted orange tree and made it grow bigger in front of all our eyes until an orange grew on it. He picked the orange, cut it open, and inside, all wet and juicy, was the person's ring.

"When I have learned how to do this," Masefield finished, "I will come to Inverness, gather the whole town about me, and produce your mother, or at least have the crowd believe I pro- duced her. Then Chris and your father can come home and live happily ever after."

At the end of the letter, he said cryptically, "I'm going to a country whence letters cannot be sent, so don't worry if you don't hear from me in a while. Love, Masefield."

That was all! Love, comma, Masefield. And this man had held Sunny in his arms! Wait a minute, there were postscripts.

The first: "You asked me how old I am: twenty-three."

The second: "About absinthe. I like the ritual of the sugar water dripping through the glass siphon and cloudying the liquor and I like the taste, but it makes you crazy drunk. I bought a Lambretta to get around in and last night, in the village square, I poured gasoline over it and tried to burn it. Luckily, every time I lit a match, an equally drunken friend blew it out. I'm told this went on for some time and several boxes of matches before we both passed out. Amazing that his breath didn't ignite the match more furiously instead of extinguish it."

"Well?" Sunny had come quietly into the kitchen. She was dressed in her father's gray terry-cloth robe, a white towel around her neck, her hair wet from the shower. "What do you think?"

"What country does this guy spy for? I hope it isn't America."

Sunny laughed. She sat down and started toweling her hair. "He doesn't say much about seeing me again, does he? Only the one reference about coming here and conjuring up Mom, and that's pretty vague. He must have learned the method from reading Daddy's books."

It was true he hadn't said he was coming and it should have made me glad but it didn't. I slumped in the chair, feeling the heart attack start up again, reverberations from the original one of Sunny's first night back, like an earthquake is always followed by some minor quakes. My main organ had become like one of those joints an old person has that acts up in certain weather or circumstances. It was something I had to live with if I was to live with Sunny. The snake. That's what it felt like each time, a snake coiling itself around my heart, squeezing it and sinking in its fangs for good measure. Mostly it was the squeezing.

The reason for this heart attack was that there was something about the letter that went beyond protestations of affection, that was better. There was a feeling of familiarity, a feeling of ongoing affection that went without saying. I felt more than ever that he would come—when, I didn't know, and when, it didn't matter.

Sunny would wait, and he would come, and I would hang around until he did, and that was the way it was.

I lifted my head to see if the clanging sound was going to start up again to accompany my heart attack, but, thank the Lord for small favors, it didn't.

Sunny just blithely went on with her hair, now brushing it. It was so fine it dried in about two minutes. It was like baby hair.

Never mind, I thought, I was the lucky one, really. Maybe he was the one she loved, but I was the one sitting here with her in the kitchen seeing her clean hair swirl around her head from the brushing. I would get to cook for her to keep her from malnutrition and be the first to see her in the morning, sleepers in her eyes and lips sort of puffed.

And who knows, maybe that country "whence" no letters could be sent was also a country whence no one ever returned from.

"Whence do you want to eat?" I asked.

# 11. IN THE BAR CENTRAL

"**M**r. Scott, sir!" I jumped to my feet where I'd been sitting by myself having a farewell *cerveza*. My vacation was over and I was off to pick up the bottom of the Iron Curtain and crawl under. Through the door of The Bar Central had just walked Sunny's father. It was an extraordinary coincidence, and yet it seems that living in the whole world as I do, these random connections become common. I put out my hand and said, "Masefield."

"Shhh." He set my chair back on its feet and pulled one up for himself. "Call me Jorge," he whispered, looking hastily around.

It was all pretty ridiculous since no one was there except Friendly Al and Paco Grande, two of the three owners, talking together, paying no attention. In the far corner, Pepe was bent over his flamenco guitar, softly strumming.

He didn't look as hunted as he was acting. It was as if he were pretending to be hunted and getting a kick out of it. "I'm traveling incognito as George Lincoln. People around here call me Jorge," he said in a more normal voice.

He was wearing gray slacks, a white broadcloth shirt, a blue beret, sandals. He looked rather dashing.

He was just as Sunny described him and as Hemingway had too. While giving every impression of a shy, benign man, he also had such a strong presence that I felt humbled, even cowed.

He looked at me severely, but it was a look of pretending to be severe, just as he had pretended to act hunted. "This is all your father's fault," he said. "He must have recommended this town to you as well as to me."

"Actually not, sir, uh, Jorge. Mr. Hemingway did. Sunny and I met him in Paris. He recognized Sunny."

"I seem to remember he was much struck by Sunny."

"I was, too."

He smiled, said, "That's good," and changed the subject. "Did you meet Count Felix Von Luckner when he was through?"

"Yes, I did." I lit up a Gitanes. The pack looked like Lucky Strikes, only green.

"He is a hero of mine," Jorge said.

I was amazed that my heroes had heroes.

"I had no idea he was still alive," he said. "One doesn't think of legends as still breathing." He smiled and added, "Do one?"

"Come to think of it, one don't." I smiled.

"But he got me in terrible trouble. I gave a party for him and antagonized some of the young rowdies, people like yourself, when I didn't invite them."

"Then you must be the one they call the Grand Old Man from Harvard who's staying at El Remo."

I had heard mention of the GOMFH from these same young rowdies. Everyone in Torremolinos had a nickname, and his was celebrated for its length. Mine was el Delgado among the Spaniards, the Thin Man, and among the others, Amazingfield.

Now Paco Grande, called so because of being much taller than the other ten Pacos in town, came over and Jorge ordered a Fundador *con sifón*. I had another beer. The three of us passed the time of day in Spanish, then Paco left us with our drinks and *tapas*—hors d'oeuvres of squid and shrimp, which Pepe brought over.

Jorge and I were both so comfortable speaking Spanish that

we continued to do so. "I kept hearing about the Grand Old Man from Harvard [*el Buen Viejo del Harvard*], but I always seemed to miss you."

"Because I avoided you assiduously. I only came to town today because I'd heard you'd departed. The soubriquet was given me by two young snots from Yale and Princeton. Now, since I didn't invite them to the party for the count, my nickname has undergone a tragic deletion."

"Yes, I heard. You're now simply referred to as the Old Man from Harvard."

He smiled. I had the feeling he was having a lot of fun here in Spain. Sunny had said he was a playful man. But it saddened me when I thought of what Sunny was going through out on that bay every day looking for her lost mother, abandoned by both her parents—and by me.

"Were you avoiding me because you were afraid I'd tell Sunny where you were," I said tonelessly, not wanting to sound accusing.

"I was afraid you would want to talk about it—which you do."

"She's not doing very well, sir."

He said, "Sunny will be fine. She's a strong girl, a good girl."

"What if she spends the rest of her life looking for Mom the way Mom looked for Andy?"

"That isn't something you or I can do anything about. I've learned that, Masefield. It took me a long time. Do you know this is the first time I've left Inverness in fifteen years? I left because I had to, just as I stayed because I had to. But now I am seeing the light on so many things. Distance, Masefield, distance.

"I have been a stupid man. I believed and sought to have others believe that the important things were Truth and Kindness. But kindness is only doing what *you* think is best for some person or people, and therefore you aren't being kind, you are being an egotist. I also believed that freedom from the ego, the self, was essential to true being. But I was a nonbeing. A nonhuman. I didn't feel!"

"What if a person *asks* you for help?" I was trying to stay with the facts, not wanting to get lost in some philosophical flight.

"That is different."

"Most times the people who most need help won't even ask."

"Masefield, I don't want to get into a discussion with you."

"And I don't want to fart around philosophizing . . . sir."

He sighed deeply and audibly, making a "huh" sound at the end of it. Intended to sound despairing, it was somehow comical. I realized the intention of the sigh must have been to show the humor of despair, just as previously he'd shown the humor of severity. Was life, then, as he saw it, essentially funny? Maybe so, but probably not. It was not very funny that his son had drowned and his wife had gone mad.

I said, "Sunny asked me to come back and help her, but I didn't because I had something I believed was more important to do. Then I came here for a week when I could have gone to her. I couldn't have done much for her in a week, but I would have been there for her. I love her. You've got to stick by your lovers when they're in trouble."

"No you don't. I stuck by her mother for fifteen years. When she lost Andy she went mad with grief, and do you know what that meant, Masefield? It meant I couldn't grieve. I couldn't shed one tear for that boy because she needed me so badly, or so I thought."

Appalled, I watched the tears well up in his eyes and spill down behind his glasses. Calm, unembarrassed, he took his glasses off, took a fresh white handkerchief from his pocket, and wiped his eyes and glasses. How wonderful to carry a handkerchief. None of my generation did. I vowed that I would. But what would I use it for? Would I have to sometimes cry? Must I mop my brow? No, I resigned the handkerchief idea. It wouldn't go with my persona—with my hoped-for persona.

He spoke in a gruff, choked voice. "Now I cry every day for Andy," he said. "All the years I thought I was being good and wise, I was being nothing, not even a man. Being kind isn't just being an egotist, Masefield, it's being outstandingly inhibited. I am not going to write anymore. I am going to drink and cry."

It's apparent that the man is having a breakdown, I thought. Probably Sunny is too. The whole family is nuttier than a fruitcake.

"You are having a breakdown, I think."

"I'm delighted to hear it. But I rather think it's a break*out*, a break loose."

"Romanticize it if you want to."

I was itching to ask about Chris, but I didn't dare. It would be too much invading his privacy. I'd gone pretty far as it was, but it had been natural concern, not curiosity, and therefore fair.

Instead I surprised myself by asking, blurting, rather, blurting it out in English, "Who is this guy, Buster?" and then I flushed. I guess, since reading about him in Sunny's letter, it had been eating away at me, all unknown.

I was appalled at my blurting. It was frightening. What if, in a sensitive situation, pretending to be a Russian or a Frenchman, I suddenly blurted into English because of thinking about Sunny. Bad action.

"Buster is a moron." Jorge also returned to English.

"Would Sunny have a such a friend?"

"He is an extremely nice moron." Jorge looked rueful. "I think it is always hard for a father to admire his daughter's lover. The first one, anyhow. The first one is the hardest."

Lover!

He looked at me admiringly and said, "Masefield, I want, just once, to be able to feel so glad and surprised that I jump to my feet and knock over my chair, or be so upset that I change languages."

I felt embarrassed. This entire conversation had been fraught with embarrassment for me, but not at all for him. I wanted to learn . . . not to be embarrassed—insouciant is the word I'm looking for—as well as invincibly uneager. I wanted to be an all-around cool guy and nonblurter.

"Such feelings are painful. Who needs them?"

"It astonishes me that a body can react so fast. My body is so slow that even if I felt like jumping to my feet, the feeling would pass before my body even began to be set in motion." He sighed his humorous sigh.

"If you hadn't looked after Sunny's mom, would she have died?"

"I guess I thought she would, but from here I see she wouldn't have because her life had meaning, even if it was crazy meaning. She couldn't die until she found Andy—although of course she could have died inadvertently while looking. But, hell, Masefield, you can't spend your life trying to avert another's inadvertence."

He paused, then said angrily with an anger that was not humorously-pretending-to-be-angry, "Because of her grieving overboard, I never got to grieve for Andy. And poor Sunny never even got to remember him."

"You sound angry at her."

"I am."

I wondered how angry. Enough to jump to his feet? Enough to have killed her?

## 12. TALKING TO MOM

One day I arrived home all drenched with bay water and fog, chattering with the cold, hoping with all my heart Buster would be there so I could tell him the news.

"Buster! Buster, I saw Mom!"

Damn. No Buster. I ran from room to room looking for him, which was silly since he'd certainly have appeared upon hearing my voice. Unless he was in the garden. He continued to care for it, to keep it going for Mom. I often found him out there. He seemed to really enjoy the work, but that was nothing new—Buster enjoyed everything he did.

I went out there but no Buster. The garden looked glorious. I think he must have been adding in plants and shrubs, for it looked quite changed. I realized that out of the corner of my eye I'd been seeing quite a lot of gardening books mounting up around the house, but I hadn't really paid attention because I never saw him read them. I knew he stayed up much later than me. That was probably when he read because when he was around me he liked to talk.

I decided it was just as well he wasn't home. He wouldn't have wanted to listen to me, looking as I did, all blue and spastic. He'd have made me take a shower first and I would have got mad at him for being such a fussbudget.

This way I could just go ahead and take a shower and get warm because there was nothing else to do.

I'd gone out on the boat on a sunny morning, dressed in shorts and a halter top, and the fog had dropped down on me out of nowhere while I was asleep, since all I seem to do these days is sail out to look for Mom, then fall asleep.

It was so pathetic—as if King Arthur or one of his knights of the Round Table went out on a quest and fell asleep on the way. That's how I thought of myself. As on a quest. A supremely important quest that the welfare of my whole family depended on, and yet, each day, it ended in being a snooze.

The shower felt great. I rubbed myself dry and put on Daddy's robe and went to the kitchen to make a cup of tea in that bowl-ish cup he had always used.

It was a week after Masefield's letter, which was still kicking around the kitchen getting grease spots on it since it was here that I'd read it and despondently left it. I'd waited to get home from the post office so the whole town wouldn't watch me read it. I'm sure they all had learned from the postmaster who and where it had come from and had gone home to look up Torre-molinos in their atlases. That's the kind of town ours was. The P.O. was the hub.

I sipped my tea and looked at the letter in its envelope, thinking of Masefield in that country "whence no letters could be sent," one of no mailboxes, no stamps. Apparently Daddy was in a similar country since he never wrote and hadn't called again as he said he would.

Suddenly in that beige colorless joyless house, sipping beige tea, I was overcome with desolation. I felt completely abandoned by everyone, even Buster. I started to cry, probably beige tears.

So, instead of Buster finding me chattering with the cold, he found me blubbering into my tea.

"Aw, Sunny," he said as he entered and looked at me aghast. "Gee whiz!" He threw off his leather jacket and came and took me in his arms. His kindness made me cry more and louder. He stroked me and hugged me and murmured comforting sounds. It was the first time we'd touched since the morning after I'd come home. He felt so big and warm and good. So good. "You've just let yourself get all run-down, champ," he said. "That's it. It's all getting to be too much for you."

"Nobody loves me!" I wailed, going for the baby routine in a big way. But did he respond by beating me about the head and shoulders and running off to the deck? No.

He said, "What do you mean? That's no way to talk. Of course they do. Everyone loves you. You're so beautiful and wonderful. You're so smart."

That made me cry harder. "I'm not at all smart. I'm completely dumb. I reverse my letters." I'd never told Buster this. Another thing Masefield knew that Buster didn't.

"You got into Cal!"

"That's meaningless. Dad got me in. And I'm not going, either." My voice was muffled from my mouth being against his shoulder.

"You're not?"

"No. Of course I'm not. It's already September and I'm not there. Hadn't you noticed? Anyhow..." I snuffled, beginning to gain control again. "Why are we talking about this?"

"I don't know. Is that why you're crying, because you reverse your letters?"

I started to laugh even though the tears were still pouring down. "Oh, Buster, I love you so much. I do."

At this, Buster's motherly stroking and comforting stopped. In an instant everything was changed between us. The blood rushed to our faces and our eyes locked as if in horror. I was struck dumb and could not protest what I knew would happen.

He lifted me up and carried me to my bedroom. He shed his clothes like a snake wriggling out of its skin, leaving it on the ground never to think about it again. It was an even simpler matter for me to drop off Daddy's robe, and then immediately our bodies were as fastened as our eyes had been a moment ago. His cock entered me and in the same motion Buster came explosively as if he'd been holding it in since my first night home and could no longer contain himself, as if the semen had backed up and I was the broken dam that allowed him release.

I didn't come but felt rocked as if by some monster wave or

shaken to the core as if I'd fallen from a great height, hitting the ground hard, getting jarred but miraculously not getting hurt. All in all, when Buster withdrew from me I felt like a survivor not a lover.

I also felt marvelously relaxed and whole and human. I felt like I'd been living in a nightmare, that I'd been in the dark underbelly of the world for the last weeks and Buster had just carried me back to the light and the life and the love . . . just in time. Not a minute too soon.

After a long comfortable silence, he asked, "What does that mean, reverse your letters?"

"Never mind. I want to tell you about today." I sat up and turned to face Buster, who lay back against the pillows like a king. A smile rested lightly on his face like sunlight spangling the water. Outside the window a swallow let forth its splattering song. Buster took one of my feet and held it in his hands like a chalice.

His eyes traced the lines of my body until I said, "I talked to Mom today," whereupon he looked at me all goggle-eyed.

"I think I was just past Hog Island, near the mouth of the bay, when I fell asleep. It was calm. I don't know how long I dozed and I thought it was the wind coming up that woke me. When I opened my eyes I could hardly see my hand in front of my face, such a fog had come in. Then I realized I was bumping up against something, another boat! Mom's boat. She was pulling away from me on a starboard tack. So, the very instant I saw her I stopped seeing her, but I knew she could still hear me. 'Mom,' I called, 'it's Sunny.' I tried to think what would be the most important thing to say since maybe I'd only be in contact with her for a minute, so I shouted, 'I'm leaving the house. I'm moving to the water cottage near the yacht club.'"

"Wait a minute. I didn't know that!" Buster interposed.

"Well, I didn't, either. That was the weird thing. But that's what I said, what I just desperately burst out with, and I knew that it was important that she know, that she have this information, so she'd know where to come and find me, when she was ready. Which I guess meant I wasn't going to look for her anymore. But here's the even weirder thing, Buster, what she said in reply. Her voice came over the widening gulf between our boats, just as clear as anything, just as true as true. She said, 'Who will look after your father?'"

It gave me chills to say it. Buster just looked at me.

"Don't you see? That means *she doesn't even know* he's gone away with Chris. She thinks she ran away and left Daddy and that he's here waiting for her like always."

Buster still didn't speak.

"Why don't you speak?"

"I don't know what to say."

"Yes you do. I know what you're thinking. You think it was a dream I had, don't you? Or you think it's what I want it to be, that I've just invented some sort of comforting explanation."

I suddenly remembered Daddy talking about his "fevered imagination" while out on the bay looking for Mom looking for Andy and almost began to doubt my story. But I am not at all imaginative. I am not the fevered type.

"Since you were asleep just before the bump that woke you," Buster offered tentatively, "it could have been a dream. Sometimes a dream carries on into the awakening and even when you think you're awake, you're not. The bump sort of goes into the dream and the dream expands on it. If you were awake, why would you say something that wasn't even true, like that you were moving to the water house?"

"Because subconsciously I knew that I was going to move there. And I am going to. I hate it here in this mausoleum. I want my own little cozy place. And even if it was a dream, which it wasn't, then it was a true dream. I said what I deep down knew was true and so did she. We both spoke from our hearts. She's worried about Dad if I leave. She knows he needs taking care of. She's always been worried about Dad. Maybe she wanted to leave him all these years but just waited for me to grow up. Maybe she's leading the life she really wants to at last."

Buster just looked at me. "How did you get home in the fog?" he asked. "How did you find your way?" I could tell that he was really curious to know this, that his motorcycle mind had taken over and wondered how a sailor deals. In a fog, a motorcycle pretty much has to stop or go really slowly. So I was proud to tell how I laid on the speed and went flying home, regardless of being blind as a bat.

"Well, since the prevailing winds are northwesterly I could tell where the northwest was, so I figured I'd go west until I hit the shore and then run south to home. It's called a beam reach. So I sailed west until I hit the shore. Since I couldn't see it, I had to physically hit it. Then I pulled up the centerboard, to get free of the mud, turned south, and ran until I saw the yacht club looming up ahead."

Buster looked impressed. Mostly, he looked to me so dear. So dear! I felt happy and lucky.

"Oh, Buster, dearest one. I feel much better. I feel free. I'm not going looking for Mom anymore. I mean, I'll go sailing still, and keep an eye out, but I'm not going to do this insane obsessive looking every day. She knows where I'll be, and since the house is right out on the water, she can sail by any time. You tell Bart, okay? You tell him I saw my mom and I talked to her and she answered back.

"And I'll tell Daddy, when he calls, to come back home. To please, please, please return. I'll tell him Mom's okay. She's doing what she wants to do and just wants to know he's being taken care of."

"Sunny?"

"What, Buster?"

"You know how you've been falling asleep so much and acting different, like crying and stuff?"

"Yes?"

"Well . . ." He cleared his throat. "I think it's because you're pregnant."

Now it was my turn to be goggle-eyed. I reacted by putting my hands to my breasts, lifting them up, and looking down at them. I hadn't had a period since Paris, but I thought it was because of all the upset of my life. I wasn't that regular anyway.

"I know your body so well, Sunny, and it's different. We'll go to the doctor and find out for sure."

He still looked like a king, but a king who'd lost his throne, who'd had it snatched from under his very eyes by intriguers at the court while he was just good-heartedly looking after his people. That's how he looked. Saddened.

His powerful body that had seemed to sing after our sudden, out-of-the-blue connection now had an elegiac stillness. For the first time, he took his eyes from my face and looked off, I don't know where he looked, just off. I lay down beside him, my head on his shoulder, pulling the covers over us, trying to make us feel safe.

# 13. A GIRL LIKE SUNNY

I stood in a doorway out of the rain watching the blearily lit cafe across the way, observing the man at the corner table who was reading a paper and drinking a glass of something dark. He was distinguished by a small red feather in the brim of his hat, a sign so subtle I'd have needed Sunny's eyes to notice it had I not been alerted.

The rain came dolefully down, making the gray stone buildings so somber that even the glistening tree leaves did not alleviate them, only seemed to wretchedly remind one of sunny days long gone. And the rain on the cobblestones made them seem slimy so that I imagined that the hissing sound of the occasional car was because of the wheels kicking up slime not water.

The street looked precarious to cross.

Which I must do at once, for the man in the red-feathered hat was getting up to go now and I had to be the first to grab his table and so make it and the newspaper mine.

He would leave by a back exit so I wouldn't see his face up close. That was the arrangement. I was not to cross the street until he got up to go.

Once inside, I saw that a woman hanging up her rain slicker on the coatrack was making for that very table. I elbowed her rudely aside and sat down, putting my arm on the paper he had left.

She was a young woman with a Slavian face: high cheekbones and slightly slanted eyes. She had an athlete's body and stance. She held herself in the way Sunny did, easy but centered, graceful but strong. You could tell that she had good reactions, quick and sure. She didn't look like Sunny at all, but she was like Sunny.

Naturally she was offended at my move. I returned her glance coldly, and although she'd started to speak, she turned away instead, sitting down at another table with her back to me.

I ordered tea since the coffee in this town was terrible.

I pretended to skim through the paper, turning pages indolently, coming at last to the classified, where an infinitesimal tear marked an ad for an apartment for rent at such an inordinate price that no one would pursue it.

I memorized the address, put a map of the city in my mind, located it. "Open between one and three," the ad said of the apartment, which meant thirteen hours or one o'clock. I had forty-five minutes.

The girl had also ordered tea.

There were three possible scenarios.

She could be any old customer wanting a corner table.

Or, somehow knowing of the plan, she could have been trying to get the paper before me.

Or, and this was the worst because if it was the correct one, I'd fallen for it and was in big trouble: she could have tried for the table just to see who would elbow her rudely aside, and by so doing get a description of me, who was in league with the other suspected man, the one in the red-feathered hat.

But it was understood that no one knew of his existence as a mole in this country. No one. He was completely safe. Which was why he refused any actual meeting with me in the transfer of information. Even now I had no idea what he looked like or sounded like.

She had looked straight at me before turning her back. My image was graven on her mind if that was what she wanted.

I would go now to this apartment and the papers would be

there, or the film of them, and I'd be out of this city by night-fall.

I'd be in Washington tomorrow and in Inverness the next day.

As long as she was just a girl who had wanted the corner table.

I could kill her to be sure. That would be a certain way to be sure that she wouldn't finger me. Radical but certain.

But if she were innocent? A young girl, little older than Sunny, an athlete . . .

"Where is the nearest phone?" I asked the cashier as I paid.

"Turn left as you leave," she said. "It is at the end of the block."

I had time. I could go to the telephone and wait to see if the girl came to use it. Or better yet, I would simply jam the phone, make it inoperable so that any attempt she made to call in my description would be futile.

This I did. It was not the most efficient way to deal with danger, but since the threat could well be only imagined, I let it lie. I passed the cafe again and saw the girl pouring out another cup of tea. I relaxed.

Not that she didn't have plenty of time to call, if they knew of the apartment and were there waiting and only needed my description confirmed.

The rain had stopped but no sun appeared to penetrate the gloom, which if anything seemed more massive—as if the day were trying to be night beforetime.

I decided to walk the twenty blocks and arrived with five minutes to spare. Everything seemed normal, i.e.: quiet and dreary, like the whole town, the whole country. The business about the girl and the feeling I hadn't handled it right was bothering the hell out of me.

What it came down to was: if the man with the feather was known to the powers that be, then I should blow this joint, not go into the building at all, hang it up. The thing could be a trap, could have been from the start. I was a catch. I knew I was a catch.

But maybe I'm being scared not smart, I thought, nervous not intuitive. The information I'm about to get is dynamic. I want to see it. I want to know what it will say. It could set off a whole series of important moves and changes so that I in my own way will have modified history. And the operation's been my baby from the start. How can I throw in the sponge at the instant of its completion?

O Mercury, patron of thieves, get me through this one and back into the sunshine, and I'll name a chemical after you, maybe a planet.

I took three deep breaths and walked up the steps to the building, then up another flight to apartment 205. The door was not locked. I turned the handle and gave it a push. It opened into a room, shabby and not very clean, which appeared to be empty. My right hand, in my overcoat pocket, curled comfortably around my Walther. I listened and it was very quiet. From the kitchenette, the refrigerator began to hum, then changed its mind. I stepped in and no one was there. Closing the door behind me, I sighed all the way down to my testicles, a sigh that Muir Scott himself could aspire to.

There was a package all by itself on the coffee table. I checked the contents, heart accelerating. They were the goods all right. I put it in my overcoat pocket, turned to go, opened the door. I stepped out.

Two men seized me, yanking my arms from my pockets, releasing both pistol and package, which a third man retrieved, pocketing them imperturbably.

The third man said, "How do you do? If you'll just come along with us, I would like to ask you some questions. We have a car waiting."

It was suddenly looking like it would be a while before I got back into the sun, or Sunny—a hell of a long while, if ever. Unless I did something.

What the hell, I thought. . . .

The men were holding my arms without stressing them, had not pulled them behind my back. With a rapid twisting motion, I freed my arms, grabbed the men by the necks, and knocked their heads together, at the same time giving one then the other a kick in the shins and throwing them at the third man and leaping for the stairs, which I plunged down three at a time.

I heard a shot, then another, but that was all right because by then I was out the door and taking the front steps in a single bound.

Unfortunately there was a reception committee—of one. One girl—shooting.

I heard the shot or maybe only felt it.

Sound and pain were one, then merged to become nothing.

# 14. THE SHERIFF

It wasn't until October that Daddy called again and we had a big fight about my not going to college. Since Daddy in his whole life has never raised his voice let alone his fist, a big fight with us constitutes one of us saying no to the other, the other saying please, the first one still saying no, and the other saying: Oh, all right, have it your own way, but you'll be sorry.

Like this: "How's everything at college? Did you find a place to live in Berkeley? What classes are you taking?"

"I'm not in college and I'm not going to college," I responded a bit sullenly. After all, why should he just *assume?* Why should he assume that I was merrily carrying out the program he'd laid down for me when he had abandoned his program of being a husband and father?

But he had other assumptions, too, which were that I didn't go because of lack of confidence inherent in being a dumbbell. "You're perfectly able to do the work, Sunny," he said. "Your dyslexia has nothing to do with your IQ."

"Dyslexia's just a fancy word for dumb."

"Tell it to Leonardo da Vinci."

"He just wrote backward so no one would try to read his journals and steal his ideas."

I could have told Daddy I wasn't going to college because of

86

being pregnant, which would be an unassailable excuse, but it wouldn't have been honest since I wasn't going to go to college regardless. I'd only gone through the motions of applying to please Mom and Dad and now that they had both cut out on me, the hell with it, I'd please myself.

"I'll no longer help you financially, then, Sunny," he said, getting all stern. "There's no point in my supporting you in a life I disapprove of."

"That's fair," I said, meaning it. Why should he pay me to go against his wishes? It meant a lot to him that I go to college. He'd been a bursary student himself and worked and scholar-shiped his way through. I knew he felt hurt and disappointed that I would scorn what he as a boy had so ardently desired.

Anyhow, I hadn't spent half of the sums he'd been sending me. I could easily last through the winter.

"I'll send you the money one more month and then you're on your own." (Through the spring!) "I hope you'll change your mind. You can still start at the winter semester. Meanwhile you can remain in the house. . . ."

I explained that I'd already moved to the water house, telling him about the foggy day I'd seen Mom and talked to her, which was now a month or so ago. "This way Mom knows where I am and can sail right up to my house if she wants. I leave out stuff for her: food, messages, warm clothes. Sometimes the things get taken, maybe by her, maybe by raccoons."

"Sunny," he persisted, ignoring my news of Mom, "education is everything in life. What will you do? What will you be? Whom will you marry? You are condemning yourself to a life with people like Buster."

That frosted me, but I thought too much of Buster to ever descend to defending him. "Aren't you even going to comment on the fact that I saw Mom?" I said stiffly.

"No." Then he reconsidered. "All right, I'm glad you saw her but I don't care about her anymore. I don't feel connected to her."

Because of this lousy response I said that which I'd vowed not to.

"Bart's going around telling people you killed Mom."

"Well, I didn't," he said.

"That's obvious, since she's alive, since I've *seen* her and *talked* to her."

"Right."

"I wasn't asking you if you'd killed her, I was just telling you about what Bart's doing. He's like the Ancient Mariner. He collars people and tells his story, even strangers."

Daddy said nothing.

"So why did you say, 'Well, I didn't'?"

"I don't know."

"Daddy, why won't Chris talk to me?"

"Because she's feeling guilty about you. She thinks she's done you an unforgivable injury. She thinks you must hate her."

I had to think about this. Had she? Did I? Since I'd stopped looking for Mom a lot of anger had surfaced, but it was pretty undirected except maybe at Buster since he was around to abuse and since he kept being so unforgivably nice to me even though I'd given him this new wound of being pregnant with little Masefield.

Then Daddy said, "I saw Masefield."

"You did!" I screeched.

"Yes. In Spain. He mentioned that he loved you."

"He did! Well, tell me," I urged manically when he didn't go on. "Tell me everything."

Daddy told me about their meeting, but he was so bad at telling things. He wasn't able to gather impressions or details. He couldn't give me any kind of picture for my mind. Maybe when you're always thinking great thoughts you don't pay attention to what's going on about you. That's why Buster was so good at telling things. He paid attention. He noticed.

"Did he jump up and knock over his chair when he saw you?"

"Yes, he did."

"Good. That means he's still eager. Did he..." I went on asking questions, but getting any information from Daddy was like pulling a person through a knothole so I gave up.

But never mind that he couldn't expand on their meeting. He'd told me the main thing. I felt so happy. "He loves me," I told little Masefield in my tummy after I'd hung up. "Your father loves me, darlin'. He told your Grampa so. In Spain."

So that's where Daddy's been all this time, I thought. It's kind of unimaginable.

I tried to place him at a bullfight or a café and couldn't. I could see Masefield enthralled by Count Von Luckner, enchanted by flamenco, agog at the bullfights, growing deranged over absinthe, but I couldn't place Daddy anywhere but here in Inverness or with anyone but Mom. I wondered where the heck he was now.

At the time of this phone call, I had been two weeks in the water house, which was one large room built on posts, set over the water at the end of a seventy-five-yard-long pier, about half a mile up the road from town. It was snug and cozy and colorful as a rainbow from quilts, rag rugs, pillows, bright-painted tables and chairs—all of which I found at garage sales or junk shops and fixed up. And books. I had books. I had started reading. Slowly, granted, but surely. Fiction. The classics. They were great. I even had Daddy's books around, although I hadn't gotten to them yet. One day Buster came in and picked up *The Question of Being* by Muir Scott and got the funniest look on his face. "What is it, Buster? You look like you've seen a ghost."

He put the book down and didn't say anything for a while, then he said, "I just got this idea." He started telling me about an idea he had for a new way of growing oysters. From strings! He was always getting ideas. Mostly they had to do with motorcycles, streamlining the chassis, or the search for a better brake. He'd invented a way to make my Franklin stove airtight so as to give me more heat, and also he moved it to a platform in the center of the room so there'd be more interior chimney pipe to heat the place. It really made a difference. Being out on the water, and with so much glass, the place got pretty cold at times. Buster wanted to put in more pipes to carry the warm air around the room and into the bathroom, but I drew the line. I didn't care to live in a boiler room, thanks.

Barthold the Bad, the Foul, the Slimey, was still making my life a misery. He didn't believe for a minute that I'd seen Mom that foggy day on the bay. He even asked the sheriff's department to drag the bay the square mile around our pier. They said if neither Mr. Scott nor his daughter had declared Mrs. Scott missing, there was no disappearance to investigate.

I got this from the sheriff himself, a nice paunchy white-haired man who came "to chat" one day. It was a boon for me that he came to visit because I got to find out about Andy.

We had a cup of coffee together, drawing our chairs up to the stove, both of us facing out to the bay, not each other. It was low tide so we looked out at mud, not water. Some snowy egrets stood around striking poses.

"I remember your brother disappearing," the sheriff said. "It must have been fifteen years or so ago. He had his own little sailboat he was allowed to use around Shell Beach as long as one of your folks was watching. And of course he always wore a life jacket. But this one day he set off on his own from the family pier. Apparently your mother had gone sailing and he was angry at being left behind so he just took off after her."

I tried to remember. Was I standing on the dock, three years old, watching Andy get into his little boat and hoist the sail, maybe saying in our secret language, "No, Andy, you're not supposed to do that. I'll tell Daddy on you," maybe seeing him get smaller and smaller in the distance, me getting scared then, and yelling, "Come back, Andy! Please come back!" Then running to tell Daddy.

But it seems like I wasn't allowed to disturb Daddy when he was working and that I was scared to knock at his door. Maybe I was scared to be alone without Andy because we were always together and he looked after me, being so big and strong and smart. Maybe I'd tried to go with him in the boat and he hadn't let me and I sat on the pier and cried my heart out and then I just fell asleep like I've always done when I'm angry or frustrated or sad, just slept there on the dock until he would come back and wake me and I'd know I was safe again with my big brother who loved me so much and understood me.

Only it was Mom who waked me, white-faced, eyes bugging out of her head, shaking me awake. "Where's Andy? The boat's not here. How long ago did he go?" shouting at me like I'd done something terrible. And I didn't know what "how long ago" was, what time was, how it was measured, especially when it was sleep time. I couldn't help, could only feel more scared, catching Mom's fear, feeling it invade my little self, me feeling this time too scared to cry or to sleep, even to speak.

Or maybe I'd gabbled away in that same baby talk I'd burst into in Paris, but what help was it if Andy wasn't there to translate?

"We couldn't get a peep out of you, poor little thing," the sheriff said. "You just hung on to your daddy and buried your face in his shirt.

"We found the little boat the next day, but we never found Andy. He had his life jacket on all right, but who knows, a shark could have got him. That was a bad year for great whites.

"We stopped looking after a week. We had helicopters and a whole flotilla of boats in the bay here. The Coast Guard patrolled the ocean side in case he could have floated out the mouth of the bay somehow.

"I guess your mom never stopped looking. It's very hard to never find the body of a loved one. There's no completion. You always wonder and hope. We knew about how she'd go sort of crazy periodically, but we respected it as family business. Private. It was for your father to handle. He knew he could call us if he wanted to.

"Now. . ." He looked at me, not the bay, looked at me hard, and his voice got hard, too. He even looked less paunchy. "I hear she's been out there a couple of months."

"That's right, Sheriff. I looked for her every day for about a month, saw her a couple of times, talked to her once. Obviously she's able to keep body and soul together, so now I just figure that's how she wants to live, that's *where* she wants to live, now that she doesn't have to take care of me anymore. Or Daddy. Probably once I went off to Paris, she thought, Now I can devote myself full-time to looking for Andy. So she's happy, I guess, in her way."

The sheriff was looking dubious, so I added, "I told her I was here if she needed me."

His brows shot up to his hairline. "You spoke to her?"

I told him yes, I definitely had spoken to her, and he asked, "What did she say when you said you were here if she needed you?"

"She said, 'Who will take care of your father?'"

"Is that so?" He relaxed and got paunchy again. "I'm glad to hear that because that somehow convinces me you really did talk with her. It's such a surprising thing to say."

"I thought so, too, Sheriff. It threw me for a loop, in fact. And since Barthold Blainey's going around accusing my father of murder, I'd like to tell you he threatened to kill Daddy if he ever came back."

"He doesn't mean much by it. He's a big noise, Barthold is. He's furious at your dad for taking his daughter away. Sees it as a personal insult."

This man's a fool if he thinks Bart's just talk, I thought sullenly. Chris and Daddy wouldn't have run away if they thought he was just talk.

"You might as well know," said the sheriff, "that Bart also says your father's been sleeping with Chris since she was a kid, that all the nights she spent with you were really with him."

"That's the biggest lie I ever heard," I said hotly. I leapt to my feet and practically jumped up and down with fury. "He's the one who tried to abuse her as a child, not my daddy. Daddy's the one who took her in to protect her from Bart." I pounded a fist into my hand. "I could kill that man."

"The murder threats are really flying around," he mused. "Well"—he got to his feet slowly—"I'll be going. Keep in touch. I'll be real interested to hear that your mother's come home when she does."

"I don't think she will until . . ."

"Until . . ."

"She finds Andy."

"And when will your dad come home?"

"I haven't any idea," I said coolly. I'd decided the sheriff wasn't a tiny bit the nice paunchy white-haired man he'd seemed.

# 15. BABY LAURIE

One day toward the end of March, Daddy called to tell me Chris had given birth to a seven-pound baby girl named Laurie.

It was a stormy day and lashes of water were streaming over the bay as if being thrown in swirling arcs from gigantic buckets. It was high tide, too, and the time of the full moon, so houses like mine were feeling pretty jeopardized. The bay was really jamming. Every so often a wave splashed up against the windows and the house shook.

I still hadn't told Daddy I was pregnant with little Masefield. I'm not sure why. I wasn't ashamed. If he could have an illegitimate child, I certainly could. I think I kept being afraid I'd lose the baby and until it was truly born, I didn't want to tell anyone.

Besides being eight months pregnant and twenty pounds bigger, other things had changed. For one thing I'd taken the postal service exam and passed it. The postmaster of Inverness was retiring and what with his pull, which I was not above using, and some help from one or two political high mucky-mucks who were retired here and were family friends, I was in line for the job.

Luckily the exam was all multiple choice and didn't require any writing. I did fine on the English comprehension and math, but there was a scary part where I had to compare columns of addresses as to which were the same. It was so easy for me, with my dyslexia, to transpose the street numbers. Then there was a section where we had five minutes to memorize a list of streets and their corresponding route numbers, and I did fine at that because I've got a hot memory. The passing score was seventy and I got seventy-six and was terribly pleased and proud. However, passing a postal service exam wasn't the sort of thing you can brag about to a Rhodes scholar, so I hadn't written it to Masefield nor did I tell Daddy now.

(I'd gone on writing to Masefield c/o American Express Paris but had never heard from him except for that one time way back in August. Even so, I was still waiting for him just as Mom was still looking for Andy and Daddy was still God knows where, hiding out.)

So, what else was new in this backwater of the world? Buster was still being the total sweetheart, taking care of me. He kept his own place but we saw each other every day and sometimes he spent the night although we weren't lovers this deep into my pregnancy. He had got every book he could find about childbirth and would read aloud to me. He wanted me to have natural birth and I thought it was a good idea too.

Another thing that happened was that Russia invaded Hungary. Masefield had been right. It was horrible. Kids my age fighting off tanks with sticks and stones. I went and picketed the Soviet embassy in San Francisco. If we knew it was coming, why didn't we stop it? Or be there to help? Maybe no one believed Masefield. Maybe Masefield worked for Russia.

Anyway, here's Daddy on the phone in March, rain pouring down, tide rising, saying he'd had a baby girl, and here's me, a passer of the postal exam and pregnant with little Masefield but still not telling.

After I heard the details of the birth, I told Daddy, while wondering where on earth she could be during this terrifying storm, "Mom's still out there, as far as I can tell, so I guess she's got through the winter all right. Now if she can just get through this killer storm we're having."

At this, Daddy just sort of grunted, then cleared his throat and said, "Chris wants to talk to you. She's right here."

"She does? She is?" I'd given up thinking of talking to her. She'd come to seem as about as accessible as Mom.

"Hi, Sunny."

"Chris!" Tears sprang to my eyes. All was forgiven. "Oh, Chris, how are you? You're a mother!"

"Sunny, she's the prettiest thing you ever saw. She looks like a little squaw. A bunch of black hair and squinty eyes."

I laughed at her idea of pretty. "Are you okay?"

"I'm fine. It was a hard birth but I'm fine now. Muir is so great. He's the most wonderful man who ever lived."

"Come home. Both of you come home."

"I want to. I miss you so much. And Inverness. In a way I even miss Barthold."

"Are you kidding? That shithead?"

"Maybe he looks different to me now that I'm a parent. He's had a hard time. He had to raise me by himself. And the drinking. It's an illness, really, you know."

This made me so mad, I forgot she didn't know the situation and said, "He's going around telling everyone Daddy killed Mom, if that's your idea of illness."

"Killed your mom?" she quavered.

"Don't worry," I said hastily, "she's not dead. I've seen her. But she's been out on the bay the whole time." Again I looked anxiously out to the bay. Not that we hadn't had plenty of bad weather all winter, but this was something else. The rain was drumming so hard on the roof, I had to shout and cover my other ear with my hand. "She hasn't been home since you guys left. Daddy didn't want you to know because of being pregnant and all."

"Oh, God."

"Never mind. I just wanted you to know about Bart so you wouldn't get some idiotic fantasy going about him."

"But I don't get it about her being on the bay."

"Talk to Daddy. He'll explain."

"I can see why he doesn't want to come back, then," she said, "with your mom acting weird, and my dad acting horrible. But even if they weren't, Sunny, I don't think he'd come back. I think he hates Inverness."

"Then why won't he tell me where he is so I can come and see him?"

"I don't know."

She must have learned to say that from Daddy, who is the only person I ever knew who could answer a question that way. It used to infuriate me when I was little and would ask him things. Then I came to admire it, figuring you must have to be really smart to not know and to be able to say so. I never came to be able to say it much myself.

Even Chris couldn't leave it simple like he could. She added, "He'll tell you when he's ready, I guess."

I noticed that a huge piece of wreckage was floating by the window and went to press my nose against the pane. At first I thought it was a smashed-up fishing boat, but no, it looked more like a piece of someone's pier.

What if it were my pier? I dragged the phone to where I could look out the front, and as far as I could tell most of my pier was gone and the rest of it was going.

I wondered how much the house was anchored in the bay by the pier. I wondered if the water house and I were about to become a gigantic piece of wreckage too. Flotsam. Well, there was nothing I could do but wait and see.

Chris was saying, "Maybe Laurie and I could at least come for a visit. We're in America now. We thought she should be born in America."

"Would you really come on a visit? Aren't you afraid of Bart anymore?" I asked wonderingly.

"No, I'm not. It's true that I thought he'd kill me if he found out I was pregnant. I was scared to death. But now that she's born, I don't feel scared. I'm not a daughter anymore. I'm a mother. He wouldn't kill a mother." She giggled.

She'd obviously completely forgotten what the man was like. Plus the fact he'd gotten worse. It was even possible that he'd gone crazy, only it would seem to dignify his behavior to say so.

"Maybe you're right," I said. "Maybe he wouldn't kill you. He hasn't actually said he would. He just mentioned he'd kill Daddy," I said bitterly, not being able to leave the subject alone. "Blow his face off into the next county, I believe his words were."

It galled me that she was so blithe. It seemed like I was left holding the bag while they were off having a gay old time.

"Oh, Sunny. I'm so sorry. It must be awful for you. You've had to bear the brunt of everything. As soon as Laurie and I are feeling strong enough, we'll come home and I'll see what I can do about Bart."

This cheered me and cleared the air.

Now I was dying to tell her I was about to have a baby too. It really was amazing when you think how we'd planned to have babies together ever since we were little and played dolls. And now it was happening—sort of—but I was constrained by the funny dread that I shouldn't tell because it might not be true and that little Masefield might die.

Still, I think I would have told her, but just when I was opening my mouth to say it, the fear smote me, the superstitious fear of jinxing the birth. And something else smote me too, the first labor pain!

Also, the phone went out.

# 16. STORM

It was a bad day for the oyster farm. The northeaster was roaring through, washing the oysters to shore, piling them up and probably smothering some hundreds under the bottom mud because of the unusual wave action. But there was nothing to do until the storm was over and we could rescatter them.

I kept thinking about Sunny. Because of all my reading about pregnancy and birth, I thought she was about ready for the baby. It had dropped some weeks ago. We'd set up a system of signaling, since the oyster farm was on Millerton Point, right across the bay from her water house, but in this storm there was no way I could see flags waving or lights flashing from her place.

Finally I just told the boss I was taking off. "I think Sunny's having her baby," I said.

I kept on my oilskins and got out the Manx from the shed where I kept it during my workday. Ordinarily it was a ten-minute ride to Sunny's house, but today it was forty-five minutes because of places the road was washed out and because of trees being down. There were mudslides too.

Then, when I got to Sunny's, her pier was out. Between me and her was only roiling water, and I know it's pathetic since I live a life surrounded by the stuff, but I am scared to death of water. There was only about a hundred yards between the shore and Sunny, but heck, that's a football field. To me it looked like two football fields with a baseball field thrown in. Probably I could wade most of the way, just bull my way through it, but at some point it was going to be over my head and then what?

Well, I could go over to the yacht club and maybe get a dory. I'd have to get over the hurricane fence they had around it to keep people like me from helping themselves to their boats, but that wouldn't be hard.

I looked at the yacht club, I looked at the water, and I have to admit I was just as scared to be out on the water in a boat. More scared. If I was going to have to mess with the stuff, I'd rather be in my own body, which I could trust more than some little vessel bobbing around at the mercy of the elements.

I stood on the shore, and even in the howling wind and rain and cold, the sweat stood out on my brow at the idea of fording through that water to Sunny. I was frozen to the spot, not by the storm but by paralyzing fear. It was a stupid fear. There was no reason for it at all. Water had never done anything to me. It was pretty to look at. Sunny loved it more than anything. She liked to say we really lived on two planets, not one—earth and water, the water one being such an alien world comparatively and full of alien creatures. Was it the creatures I feared?

The water house didn't have windows looking to the shore except for a little porthole one in the bathroom, which from here was no help in finding out if Sunny was even there—and I would have seized on any sign to persuade myself she wasn't— but she could look out and see me and she must have because, suddenly, she appeared by the door on the part of the pier that was still standing. She had the "I'm in labor" flag in her hand and a rope and lifesaver in the other, which she let fly.

The baby was on its way!

It was all I needed to galvanize me into action. I strode into the water, the mud sucking at my boots. For a minute I couldn't see anything and then I realized I had closed my eyes. When I opened them I saw that Sunny was still letting out the rope attached to the lifesaver. I hoped it was a long one. The waves were carrying it toward me, although every so often it would switch directions.

I kept going, closing my mind to the fear now (instead of my eyes), just thinking of Sunny and the baby coming. The water was to my waist now and chest. Yellow foam and flotsam covered the surface. I muscled my way on. I felt I could walk through stone to get to Sunny if I had to.

Then I was toppled by a wave and went under. I struggled upright, gagging out the mouthful of water. I regained my footing only to go down again. This time I kept my mouth closed. I started to panic but talked myself out of it. Cut it out, I told myself. Grow up. Stop being a baby. You're being a chicken. Stop being a baby chicken. What can it do to you? It's only water. But that's *why* I'm so scared. Because it's water! Tell me, what's so bad about water? I don't know! Help!

But the next thing I knew, I was moving through it in a different way. On top. I was kicking my feet and moving my arms and, because my face was in the air, I was breathing air. This is swimming, I realized. This is what they call swimming. I know how to swim. It's a miracle.

I grabbed the lifesaver and Sunny started hauling me in. I reached the ladder that was attached to the pier on the bay side of the house and clambered up. I stripped off my clothes outside so I wouldn't puddle up the house, all the time thinking, The baby's coming! The baby!

Inside Sunny had a towel out for me and I stood by the stove drying myself off while she found some sweats for me to put on.

"Did your water break?" I asked her.

"No, but the pains are coming fast and regular. Buster, what'll we do?"

"Why, I'll deliver him for you, of course. I've read all about it. There's nothing to it."

I went over to the kitchen sink and started scrubbing my hands like crazy. Now that I'd crossed through water, anything else seemed simple. It was Sunny's turn to be scared, with the sweat on her brow. Only she was in pain too. Poor Sunny. I knew how she felt. The unknown. But she'd find out she could swim too.

"Don't be scared, champ. Don't be a baby chicken."

"A baby chicken?" she said wonderingly.

I laughed and explained, "That's what I was telling myself when I came through the water."

"Do you realize that you were swimming, Buster?"

"It was a miracle."

"No, it wasn't. It means that you learned when you were a kid, in those forgotten years of yours. Yikes!"

"Put a bunch of towels down on the bed and lie down. Time your pains. Are you sure your water didn't break?"

It hadn't broken because little Masefield (How I hate that name. How Sunny could saddle her baby with a name that his father must have gotten somehow by mistake, and keep the mistake going just out of obstinacy, beats me) was a caul baby, which is a baby born while still in its bag of waters. It's a magic baby. They say caul babies are bound to have some kind of special gifted graced life from being born that way. And it was such an easy birth for Sunny. She was only in labor about two hours or so and then that little kid just slipped out in his bubble of water.

When he first appeared I saw this baby's head all rainbow colors like a jewel—an opal or moonstone—and I thought, What's going on here? The water was creating this effect. It was beautiful.

Then I realized I had to break the bag of waters right away so he could breathe, so I bit it open and got a mouth full of saltwater for the second time that day. Then I cleaned out his tiny nostrils and mouth with my fingers.

"It's a boy, Sunny."

"Aren't you supposed to turn him upside down and slap him, Buster?" Sunny asked anxiously.

"Why, no, honey, he's breathing just fine. We've just gentled him into the world and he's going to have a blessed life. At least he would have if he didn't have to carry a terrible burden of a name like Masefield. Won't you change your mind about it?" Now I was cutting the umbilicus that bound mother to son, their first separation.

"Masefield is his father, Buster." She said it in that voice she gets when she's also saying, "Don't get your hopes up. Remember that Masefield is the one I love, not you." "This is his son," she said.

It wasn't as harsh as it sounds. That kind of talk of Sunny's didn't bother me that much anymore. The pain no longer tore up my middle from my balls to my brain, it only sort of snagged my heart like a fish hook. Because I didn't believe it. It was just a habit she had of talking like that and saying that sort of thing. She'd probably still be doing that when we both were in our eighties—out of the same habit and because she's so repetitive.

She hadn't even heard from the guy except for that one letter early on, the one I helped myself to. I figured she wouldn't have left it lying around the kitchen if she hadn't meant me to see it. He didn't say anything about how he loved her and missed her and wanted to see her. He didn't say one thing about her being the most glorious creature that ever walked the earth. He just bragged on about the great time he was having and didn't seem to mind portraying himself as a complete adolescent fool.

It's true that the letter bothered me, made me realize the guy existed and that he did care about Sunny in his way, but then a little time went by and Sunny and I were being so much like a young married couple, with the baby coming and all, that I just stopped worrying about him. Especially since he never wrote again.

"You can't even make a nickname out of it," I went on complaining to Sunny, "unless you'd want to call a boy Maisie."

Sunny smiled. She gave me a really loving look.

I sighed. "Okay, I'll just call him M, I guess. Well, little M, welcome to the world. Come meet your mom."

I put him in Sunny's arms and then tended to receiving the afterbirth. That done, I just looked at the two of them and I couldn't help myself. I started to cry. What a beautiful sight they were, mother and babe.

I went to the bathroom, where I could cry in peace and not disturb the two of them. Even so, I was blubbering away so loud they probably heard me. It was a reaction probably from the strain of getting through the water and then the birth—both things. But it was also because I felt so happy, so lucky!

I took a leak while I was at it, then washed up and blew my nose before going back to Sunny and M, to my family.

The storm had calmed and the little house no longer rocked and shuddered with every wave. The tide had lowered, the wind dropped, and there was only the steady patter of rain on the roof—a good sound. I stoked up the fire and tidied up. Then Sunny said she wanted to sleep, so I took little M from her and sat up the rest of the night with him. I held him in my arms the whole time to be sure that he was a survivor, and with the passing of hours I could feel us grow bonded to each other. Not that I wouldn't have loved any kid of Sunny's, but as far as feelings go, little M is my son and I'm his daddy. He's flesh of my flesh from this night of birthing him and holding him.

# 17. EYEWITNESS

Three months after Laurie was born, Muir told me to
go back to Inverness. "I'm not a fit companion for you," he said.
"You should be with people of your own age, especially Sunny.
You should be back in the town that you grieve for and settle
down, make a home for yourself and Laurie. You are a girl who
likes being settled. I am a nomad, an *old* nomad."

At this point in time we were at the apartment of a friend of
his in Boston, Massachusetts. It was a stifling hot humid day.
Looking out the window, I saw endless brick buildings. The
town was like a kiln. Here and there were some leafy green
trees, but I'm a pine tree kind of girl myself and preferably, if
something's got to grow out of the ground around me, give me
grass. Muir was right. I was damned homesick. I longed for the
high grassy hills of Point Reyes, speckled with holsteins, and the
cool glassy bay reflecting the cows, hills, sky, and anything else
going on. I wanted to feast my eyes on gulls, cormorants, pelicans, and pipers. I thought I would scream if I saw another
pigeon. I was sick to death of cities and sweat and traffic and
traveling. I thought if I had to pack our bags one more time, I'd
put a bullet through my head.

And yet, I couldn't leave Muir. I loved him. Maybe it isn't
normal to love a man so much older, but screw it, I did, and

those were the facts of the case and anyone who didn't like it could go fuck themselves sideways as far as I was concerned. Except for Muir. He was one of the ones who didn't like it, but I didn't want him to fuck himself, I wanted him to fuck me.

Which he never had.

So I said, "You're right. I want to go back to Inverness. I'm desperate to see Sunny. But just for a visit. If it means leaving you forever, forget it." I lifted my hair. Even in braids it was too heavy and hot to bear. I decided right then to cut it all the hell off. Why was I dragging it around all these years? What did I think it was, a national treasure, something I had to preserve for the ages? It was just hair. It grew back, like fingernails. It wasn't a limb. "I'm going to cut my hair."

"Good."

I laughed. "Anyone else would say, No! No! Your beautiful hair, how could you!"

"You're avoiding the subject."

"I am not. I just told you I'm not going unless I can come back and that's that."

"No, it isn't," he said.

What he meant was that isn't always that, not all of the time, and especially not this time, because before the week was out Laurie and I were home—driving into Point Reyes Station in a rented car—and Muir wasn't having me back and wasn't telling me where he was going next.

It was over. He took care of me while I carried Laurie. He waited until she was born and we both were okay. Then he cut me loose.

He never pretended he was going to do any different, but naturally I'd allowed myself to hope he'd get attached to me. Well, he hadn't and that was that and now I was home and there was a lot to be said for coming home. The closer I got, the better I felt.

I drove over to the house where I'd lived with Dad. Not that I was going to stay there. I had plenty of money, thanks to the generosity of Muir, and I would probably just stay at the inn until I found a place of my own. Not that I wanted to see Dad, either. I was dying to drive right to Sunny and surprise her, but I just figured I'd better see what was what around here before I made any decisions.

The place was a complete pigsty. It probably hadn't been cleaned the whole year since I was gone. I had to hide Laurie's face because I figured that even at three months it would make a terrible impression on her little growing personality. Luckily she didn't know it was her grandfather's. Even so, she started to cry, probably because of the smell. I walked back to the car and leaned against it, drawing in the sweet fresh air and watching a red-tailed hawk fly circles around some lesser birds.

I began to straighten out my thoughts and decided that maybe Dad's brain was in the same shape as his house and I might be jeopardizing my baby. I should see him first alone, without Laurie.

I walked a few blocks to the *Point Reyes Light,* the world's tiniest newspaper, where a dear old friend might be found, being a self-proclaimed news gatherer when she wasn't being a mid-wife, knitting sweaters, or keeping bees and selling their honey to the markets.

She was there. I left Laurie with her and gathered the news that Dad could be found right now at the saloon; she'd just noticed him go in.

Outside the bar, I asked a kid who was loitering about to get my dad to step outside. "Tell him it's his daughter." I didn't want to walk in and give him a shock. I thought it would be a good idea to prepare him.

As the boy went through the door I heard "Your Cheatin' Heart" coming from the jukebox. Hank Williams.

Then Bart stepped out. He looked the same, really. His clothes were okay: the fly was zipped and the buttons buttoned. His hair was cut and fairly combed. Maybe he was a little thinner. Maybe his eyes weren't quite focused. He wasn't drunk. I could always tell at a glance if he was and in what stage. But his eyes were... funny. They made me real nervous. I could feel chills at the back of my neck.

"So it's you," he said.

"Hi, Dad. I'm back," I said, trying to sound easy in my mind.

"Let's go sit down on the bench over there and talk."

"I got nothing to say to you."

"Well, then, maybe you'd like to listen." I went over to the bench and he followed me, stiff-legged in the way that horsemen walk, only more so.

"How's everything?" I asked.

"I lost my job." He squinted his eyes at me as if he were looking at me from a distance.

"I'm sorry to hear that."

He brushed away my words like they were so many flies and asked, still squinting, "What'd you go away for?"

"So I could have my baby in peace and quiet and safety."

He looked down at the ground and spat. "I wouldn't hurt your kid."

"I know you wouldn't. But you might have hurt me while I was carrying her."

"I don't do that stuff anymore. I stopped drinking."

"You did? That's great, Dad. That's really good. I'm proud of you."

"I don't want no fucking medals. It's no big deal."

I realized I was talking to him as if he were a little kid, or some kind of dummy. He'd always been so mean and scary, but now he *was* like a little kid. But did it make me feel glad and relieved? No. I felt nervous.

"I stopped drinking because no one believed me."

"No one believed you about what?"

"And they still don't, but I'm sticking to my story and someday they'll see I was right. Trouble is, sometimes I still act drunk even though I'm not. That's something that happens. It all comes back on you from inside your brain and you act all drunk and crazy even if you haven't been drinking. So everyone thinks I still drink. I lost my job. And I lost my daughter."

"Well, I'm home now, Dad. Me and Laurie. We're back to stay. But I'm getting my own place."

"Just because he wrote some book and has a big house, everyone believes him and not me."

"Believes what?"

He looked off, his eyes vacant. He talked tonelessly, as if he'd

said the words so many times they were just sounds to be repeated. "They all believe he didn't do it. How much proof do
you need? You got the fact that he left town and no one knows
where he is, not even his own daughter, and you got the fact
that his wife has disappeared from the face of the earth and
you've got me, an eyewitness."

"If you're talking about Muir Scott," I said waspishly, getting
mad as a swarm of them, "you've also got me, who knows where
he is and knows he left town because he couldn't stand it here
another day and couldn't handle his wife anymore. I went along
with him because I was pregnant and scared and begged him to
take me. He was kind enough to oblige."

Dad just looked off and went on talking as if he hadn't heard a
word. Everything he said made me want to rip his throat out,
but I held my tongue. I figured I should hear the whole story
so I'd know what he'd been telling everybody and see how to
proceed.

"He's rich and educated and everyone says how good and wise
he is. Crap! Wasn't he the kind one, they say, to take Chris into
his home and save her from her drunken father. All the time he
was poking her. Finally he gets her pregnant and then what's he
going to do? What about all those people who think he's such a
saint? And what about his wife? Well, he don't need to worry
about the wife if she never knows what hit her, does he? So he
bumps her off and leaves town with my kid, who doesn't even
know what he's done or she'd never have gone with him. He
tells his own daughter her mother's out on the bay just sailing
around having a fine old time, and the poor kid spends every
day looking for her and even swears she's seen her, tells everyone
she's talked to her so people can keep on thinking I'm crazy and
don't know what I seen with my own eyes."

"What did you see?"

He was silent.

"Well, what did you see?"

"I never told anybody what I saw. I just said I knew he'd killed
her and I do. And I said I'd kill him when he came back and I
will."

"Why?"

"Why?" He turned to me and brought me back into existence. I'd begun to think I wasn't even there. I wished I weren't, too. "What do ya mean, why?" he asked angrily.

"What did Muir Scott do to you that you want to kill him?"

"I just told you," he said, raising his voice. "He took my kid away. And made me look like I was crazy. Now I've stopped drinking to show them I know what's what and what I saw."

"Well, your kid's back. Here I am. See. Look at me. I'm here. And my baby, Laurie, is here, too. And we're doing just fine and I suggest you stop going around saying you're going to kill Muir Scott for no reason and then maybe people will treat you better and you'll feel better and it would certainly be a kindness to Sunny, who's my best friend in the world. How do you think it makes me feel, your behaving this way?"

"They should know the truth," he insisted.

"The truth is that Muir Scott is not the father of my baby and he never slept with me once."

That was the exact truth of the matter. I just hoped everyone else around here didn't think Laurie was Muir's baby too. Did Sunny? Lord!

"I don't even know who the father is and I don't care. But I do know that it isn't him and it isn't you, although it could have been when I was younger."

I figured a little blackmail might help around now, help straighten things out, bring a little order to the situation by maybe scaring the shit out of him.

"That's not true," he said flatly. "I never did."

"Yes you did. And if you're so interested in the truth of things, you better face up to that. Maybe you don't remember because of the drinking. Maybe you conveniently blacked out every time. But it happened and it's the truth. So I have my truth I can tell the whole two towns if I want to bring more shame on us."

Squinting his eyes again, he bent toward me, lowering his voice, practically whispering, and it was horrible what he said. Horrible!

"I seen him scuttle the boat," he said. "Her boat. I seen him tow it out into the bay and sink it."

# 18. P.O.

"See you tomorrow!" I waved off the mail truck and threw the sacks into my office: one full of magazines and bundles and low-class mail, the other sack with a lock on it containing the first-class mail. It was a hot, still September day. Across the street, the bay was glistening in the early morning sun. This working all day sure tore into my sailing time, but I loved the job.

Here came Buster and little M down the street from the market, holding hands, munching on huge sugar doughnuts. The two inseparables. "Hey, you guys, M should be at school by now," I called out.

"He's going to come to work with me today."

"Oh, Buster, you're always taking him to work."

"Please, Mom! It's the first day of the harvest because it's such a low tide."

"Little kids love mud," said Buster. "You can't deny him a morning in mud, oystering away."

Masefield was four. He had my straight blond hair and Masefield's violet, black-lashed eyes. He was built like a spider monkey, all arms, legs, and fingers. He was always waving his arms around and he held his fingers straight out, not curled, so they looked long and innumerable. Except when he was walking along, holding Buster's hand, he ran everywhere so that it always seemed there was a puff of dirt and dust behind him like a cartoon character.

He was the sweetest little boy who ever lived.

"Okay, M, honey," I said.

I always gave in to them. Heck, it was only a preschool, he wouldn't miss anything, except Laurie. Laurie always got mad and upset when M didn't come to school.

Here came Chris and Laurie from the other end of the street, having walked down the hill from their cottage in the woods. Chris worked in the restaurant, being everything from cook to busboy, and she was taking classes at College of Marin. She had cut her long hair into almost a crewcut and now it was Laurie who had the long black braids looking like Chris did when I first knew her.

Our dream plan had come true; our children were growing up together and loved each other. We were equal mothers to them both, but Buster, while always sweet to Laurie, was only one kid's father.

"Hi, Chris," I called, always so happy to see her, even though it was not a rare occurrence, happening as it did several times a day. "Hi, Laurie, honey," I called to my girl-child.

I left the four of them talking in the middle of the main street and ducked back into my office to don my rubber thumb and poke up the mail.

When Chris came back that year our babies were born, we suckled them interchangeably. All that summer long we'd sit on the deck of the water house, babes to our breasts, talking talking talking, our eyes involuntarily sweeping the bay for Mom.

Chris had come back because she wanted to, but also, as she told me at our first talk, "to set things right."

"When you told me over the phone about your mom out on the bay and about Bart going around saying Muir had killed her so he could run off with me, I knew I had to come back because I'd left the totally wrong impression, selfish and careless bitch that I am, and done horrible harm to you and your family."

"What do you mean, Chris?"

"I mean that Laurie isn't your dad's baby," she told me. "I don't even know whose she is. I was so messed up, Sunny, even you, my best friend, didn't know how sick. I didn't want you to, either. Oh, you knew I was wild, but not that I was crazy. I was sleeping with so many guys it was like I had a bet on or like I was trying for some kind of record. But never with your dad. Not once. Not that I wouldn't have if he wanted me. But it's thanks to him I have any kind of respect for men. Him and Buster, too, who's good as gold.

"When I got pregnant, I was scared shitless of what Bart would do if he found out, but even more scared to get an abortion. I went to your dad like I'd done so many times before. I told him I was going to kill myself. He said he was going away and would take me with him. But what will people think? I asked. He said he didn't care. Let them think what they wanted to. We went away that night."

"How is Daddy?"

"He cries a lot."

"Really!" I exclaimed. "How strange. He was always so happy."

"No he wasn't. Not deep down. I knew that already. That's why we always understood each other so well and why I could go to him. He says he's glad to be able to cry."

"But what is he crying *about?*"

"He says he's crying for Andy—at last, after all the years— but I think he's crying for your mom."

Then I told her that little M wasn't Buster's baby but Masefield's. She listened, then she said, "You were carrying the baby of the man you loved, living with the man you didn't, and it was the opposite for me, living with the man I loved, with some stranger's baby in my womb. Isn't life too weird for words?"

"But I do love Buster, you know. I'm just not *in love* with him."

"I know," she said, getting such a fond expression on her face I knew she was thinking of all the times I'd said it, each time as if it were the first.

"As for Bart," she said, "I'm simply not afraid of him any-more. I told him that unless he shuts up about this whole thing,

I'm telling everyone this baby's his. It could be, too. He never did fuck me, but it wasn't because of not trying. Of course I couldn't really tell people that—it wouldn't be fair to Laurie. But the idea didn't even seem to rattle him. He's obsessed about your father and I'm afraid there's going to be no shutting him up. If threats don't work, I'll try money. What a mess. My dad and your mom are a couple of beauts. I hope we don't end up a pair of loonies too."

"Would you really want to marry Daddy?" I asked, trying to envision them together.

"I'd lie down and die for Muir. I came back because I had to set things straight, but I want to stay with him forever. He said I should be with you now and raise the baby here. He said he had to be alone and think about things. I begged him to let me come back but he said no. Now, even I don't know where he is. I've lost him."

Being an Indian is like being a champ; you don't cry easy. But I saw two big tears squeak out of her eyes like they were made of stone and roll down her face as if they were cutting into her cheeks. Then she scrinched up her face real tight and that was the end of them, just the two.

Now it was four years later and I was casing the mail on a beautiful September morning, the street outside full of people I loved: Buster and M licking the sugar off each other's fingers, Laurie pulling Chris over to the market, probably to get some doughnuts for themselves. Gradually a crowd was forming around Buster as usual, people passing the time of day but also asking him, How do I do this? Some problem with their car or hot-water heater or leaky roof and Buster telling them how to deal with it and like as not promising to come on by later to give them a hand (helping out with one hand, refusing any money with the other).

Daddy was still hiding out and I would hear from him once in a blue moon. And Mom? She was still out there, only it wasn't a private family matter anymore. She'd become sort of a legend like the Loch Ness monster and people would pride themselves on having seen her and it would always hit the local papers when somebody did: the *Point Reyes Light* or the *Coastal Gazette*.

Practically from the day he was born, I took little M out on the bay with me. Of course I wanted him to grow up loving the water, but also I wanted Mom to see she had a little boy grandchild that she could love so she'd maybe give up looking for Andy. But, heck, I guess if being able to love me when I was little didn't stop her, little M wasn't going to, either.

One time I came home from a sail and I heard little M ask Buster, "Where's Mom?"

"Out looking for Mom," he said.

"Oh," little M said unconcernedly, and I realized that it is in this way that situations so weird and crazy become natural and second nature and just taken for granted.

Except that I was sane. I was looking for Mom because I knew she was out there, didn't I, whereas she, deep down in her sanity, knew Andy wasn't. That was the difference between us. Wasn't it?

As for Bart, Chris's plan to threaten him into silence didn't work at all. Instead of silencing him, he got worse. He completely disintegrated, lost his job and hit the streets, or roads, rather. He'd be seen wandering from town to town telling his story to whoever would listen, how Muir Scott, the famous philosopher, had seduced his child away from him when she was only an adolescent and then, having gotten her pregnant, took her away entirely, after having first brutally murdered his wife. Bart now went so far as to say he'd seen Daddy do it. "*I seen him scuttle the boat,*" he told people. "*I seen him in the dark of night, in his dory and outboard, towing her one-design into the bay and scuttling it.*"

He was the scum of the earth and there was nothing whatsoever we could do about it.

I unlocked the first-class mailbag and cased up the thirty or forty letters. I have to admit that even after all this time, I never opened that sack without wondering if there'd be a letter from Masefield. Sometimes I wondered if I didn't get the postmistress job so I could be the first in the sack, so that no one in town would see his letter before I did.

One time, after M was born, I got Masefield's family's address from Daddy and wrote them to inquire about him. His father answered that he didn't know where he was but the nature of his work kept his whereabouts secret even to them.

His was obviously a family that didn't go looking for their lost ones.

Today, the first-class sack tossed up a letter for me. It was from Europe, but it wasn't in his handwriting. Still, I knew it would have to do with him because of the foreign stamps. With trembling fingers I opened it and inside was another envelope, all ragged, smeared, and torn, addressed to me by Masefield. My finger-shaking revved up so bad I could hardly open this one, then when I did, I could hardly read it through the tears. It was written in pencil on a scrap of some very rough paper. "My darling Sunny, If this letter gets through to you, then I will too. I'll be seeing you soon. Masefield."

Outside, a rare car driving through dispersed the group. People went off to begin their day. Buster got on his bicycle—he'd given up his motorcycling for the sake of M's safety—M on a seat on the back that Buster had made specially, holding on to Buster's belt.

Looking my way, they both smiled and waved good-bye.

I held up a hand, but it didn't move, just stayed palm out motionless, as if I were taking a vow.

# 19. THE TRAMP

It was a September evening. I dined alone at my Hamburg house on roast chicken. My man suddenly appeared at the table. "Excuse me for interrupting, Count, but there is a tramp at the door who will not go away. He says you know him."

"A tramp, eh?" This was very interesting. I knew something about tramps, having been one myself. I pushed away my plate.

"He insists on seeing you. I tried to drive him off but he stood firm."

"Does he have a name, this tramp?"

"He is extremely hard to understand and he is . . . unsightly." His face signified that his smell was offended more than his sight.

I fell into a reverie, thinking: Yes, I had been a bum once, a miserable creature to drive off from the door. You feel completely ashamed and humiliated even though you know in truth you are a godlike youth and not at all the wretch you appear. Only unexpected circumstances have temporarily matted your hair, stubbled your chin, stunk up your body, and dirtied your clothes. Only chance events like hurricanes, imprisonment, or theft have made you so hungry you're ready to beg on your knees for a crust of bread. A man appreciates a little kindness at such times.

It was when I was a teenager and ran away from home to sail before the mast. As well as being hungry and dirty, I was dragging around a broken leg without a cast, having been kicked out of the hospital for lack of money.

I'd broken my leg in a hurricane. What a blow that was. The foremast went overboard, the topmast followed. Combers swept over the ship, breaking everything to pieces, including the men. The steerage deck broke and the ship began to leak. We pumped until we were worn out. Then a gigantic wave broke over us and six men were swept away from the pumps. Three went overboard; the others were dashed against the shrouds. I braced myself between two timbers on the deck, but the breaker drove them together and pinned my foot. I fell and my leg snapped.

"Shall I give him the boot?"

Who was this man standing at my table and what was he talking about? Oh, yes, the unsightly tramp at the door.

I held up my hand, wanting to finish my thoughts because I realized I had the wrong story, by Joe, the wrong broken leg.

The hurricane leg had just knitted up when darned if I didn't break the other one just above the ankle. I was sailing on a schooner bound from Nova Scotia to Jamaica with a cargo of lumber. We were in the harbor, discharging the cargo, when . . .

Yes, I broke my ankle that time, but was that the time I got thrown out of the hospital? I know I had no monies because that unspeakable captain had sailed away with everything I owned. I had only the rags on my back. I slept on the beach. . . .

"Count, what shall I do about this tramp?"

Blast the fellow. He doesn't give me a minute to think. I beetled my brow, saying, "Show him in, of course! The man maintains he knows me. Who are we to doubt his word?"

"If you say so, Count."

I recognized the gallant young Masefield when I saw him, although he was changed since our happy days in Torremolinos. He looked like he'd been through a thing or two since; one thing had aged him a decade, the other had knocked the stuffing out of him. Not to mention that he was in that stage of emaciation when the body is eating its own muscles and nerves. I could tell the boy was at the end of his tether and involuntarily got to my feet to catch him when he fell.

The last strand of his will that had held him together long enough to get to me now gave way. "I escaped," he said. "Just as you did."

Motuihi, he meant, the New Zealand island I escaped from when a prisoner of war in 1914, but that was a lark! Unlike this boy, I was in fine health and strength for that endeavor. But never mind that now. The boy was about to fall.

Yes. Having spoken, Masefield began his collapse and I was there to catch him as planned.

"By Joe! Let's get the boy to bed. Heat up some milk and call the doctor. He's half-starved to begin with and half-dead as well. We'll just have to hope he's not half-mad, too, as that's harder to remedy."

That's the way it is. It's when you finally get help that you give up and die. I remember my six days adrift in the lifeboat, our ship having gone down in that hurricane of the first broken leg, and just when the implacable moment had come for drawing straws to see whose blood we'd drink, all of us feeling pretty reluctant to drink or be drunk, we sighted a steamer. It bore down upon us, dropped rope ladders for us to climb aboard, but for our lives we couldn't move a muscle, couldn't blink an eye. They had to get out their cranes and hoist us aboard like bales of cargo.

I carried the boy up to bed. Pretty good for an octogenarian. Of course, he was only skin and bones and soul.

Masefield stayed with us six weeks. He put on some flesh and lost some years—except in the eyes. His eyes stayed sunken—cold and dark.

At his request, I taught him the Indian fakir magic. He was very adept. I brushed up my own skills while I was at it and together we improved on what I knew.

I told him all my stories, but he didn't tell any of his, not one. He would not even tell me where he had been imprisoned, or by whom, or how he got away.

Once he said, "Like you, Count, I want to participate in the history of the world. I want to live in the whole world, not just a town or even a country or continent. I want to be a part of the whole thing, an important part."

"Ah, but what is the good of it, my boy," I asked wonderingly, "if you can't regale the world with stories about the part you play? For me that has been most of the fun of it, and to have fun, you know, is the main idea."

He thought about that and said, "We are different personalities. You have always gloried in your exploits, in being a hero, a legend. But with me, it isn't that I want to be known, it's that I want... *to know*."

## 20. HAVING A COLD

One late October morning, I woke up in Sunny's water house with a terrible cold. I'd had it for a few days, but this morning it was ten times worse. My throat was sore, my glands were swollen, my nose was completely stuffed. My head was killing me. I felt horrible.

Whenever I got sick, Sunny was totally unsympathetic. The thing was, she never got colds, never got colds or flus or anything. She had some kind of incredible immune system. Little M knew a thing or two about colds, but sympathy from a little kid isn't the same. M's so cute when he says "poor Buster" that instead of feeling better because someone cares if you live or die, you just think how cute he is.

"Aren't you going to get up, Buster?" Sunny asked from the kitchenette, all matter-of-factly as if it were a normal day and I could breathe like a normal person.

"No," I answered, only it sounded like dough.

"You mean you're not even going to go to work?"

"Dough."

M came over to the bed and snuggled under the covers next to me. "Poor Buster," he said, "you're so sick."

"I dough."

"Are you really going to stay in bed?"

The kid was impressed.

"Yes. My throat hurts. My nose is so stuffed I can hardly breathe. Sunny, you remember how yesterday it was my left nostril that was so stuffed?"

"Yes."

"Well, today my right nostril is the worst. They're both bad, but today my right nostril is completely stopped up."

"Yeah?"

"Yes. It feels like it has cement in it."

"Golly."

All her responses were completely automatic and uncaring. I could tell she wasn't even a tiny bit interested in my symptoms. "How do you suppose the body just keeps making all that snot?" I asked her, really wondering. "I mean, I must have blown my nose a hundred times in the night." She, of course, had slept through the whole thing.

"It's like tears," she said. "Sometimes, when you cry, it's unbelievable that all that water can just keep coming and coming. Where does it come from? How can there be so much? you wonder."

I remembered that Sunny had sometimes cried.

It cheered me up to remember that at least she had cried, even though she'd never had a cold. "I know, Sunny, but tears are water. Snot is . . ." I wasn't sure what snot was.

"Snot is icky," M said, making his solemn contribution. We started to laugh our heads off.

"It's gucky, too," I said.

"It's icky-gucky," said M.

The laughter got me coughing and I couldn't breathe. I struggled for breath. Couldn't get it. It was like that time under the water when I was going to be with Sunny to birth little M, only worse.

My hands scrabbled the air for something to hold on to. Something to breathe. Sunny just said, "M, come on over here away from Buster. You're going to get his germs. Come and finish your breakfast."

Just before I died from lack of oxygen, a breath struggled through all the snot and phlegm and I survived. I collapsed back down on the bed, dragging in gulps of air.

"Buster's just being a baby chicken," she told M. "Men are such babies when they get colds. They're so self-pitying. Men can't stand any kind of pain or discomfort," she went on with her false indoctrination. "Whereas we women are tough. If men had to go through labor pains, no babies would ever be born."

"Don't listen to her," I gasped. "She doesn't know anything about labor pains. She had the easiest birth under the sun. You just swooped out in a magic bubble, M. She didn't feel a thing."

"Buster's my daddy," little M told Sunny. It made me grin to hear it, even though I was feeling so awful.

Sunny had carefully taught him that his real daddy, the man who put the sperm in her to make the baby, was a man named Masefield, who was his true father and who would come home someday. She wanted him to know the truth from the start, and from the start, as soon as he could talk, he denied it, claiming me as his true daddy. Sunny blamed me for this, but I had never contradicted her story and she knew I hadn't. Whenever M wanted to get her goat he'd say how I was his real daddy.

Now Sunny was putting on her postal uniform. "Don't leave me," I wailed.

"I'm staying with Buster," Masefield told her.

"You are not. You're going to school."

"Dough," he imitated me, collapsing in giggles.

Sunny brought me some fresh-squeezed orange juice and some aspirin. "You'll be okay, Buster. I'll come back and give you some hot soup for lunch."

I sat up to drink the juice, plumping the pillows behind me. "My nostrils . . ." I began.

"I don't want to hear any more about your nostrils. It's too boring. Take your aspirin and sleep. You'll feel better. Look, it's a beautiful day. Maybe we can have lunch out on the deck, in the sun."

"What if I die before lunch?" I asked piteously, remembering my coughing spasm.

"Is Buster going to die?" M asked Sunny.

"Now stop it, Buster. See how you're scaring little M."

"Is he?"

"You can't die from icky-gucky disease," she told him, and started laughing her head off. They both went off laughing to beat the band and probably didn't think another thing about me. I fell asleep.

I woke up because someone was knocking at the door. I hauled myself out of bed. "Hold on, I'm coming." I dragged on a pair of sweatpants and staggered to the door, wondering who in heck it was since our friends always just knocked and walked in. I grabbed a paper towel and opened the door, blowing my nose. This guy stood there I'd never seen before. "Hi, come on in," I said, holding wide the door. "What can I do for you?"

"I'm looking for Sunny Scott. Someone directed me here."

He was tall and thin and was, I suppose, actually what you might call a great-looking guy. He was Masefield. I was sure it was him. He'd come just as Sunny always had said he would. And here I was, blowing my nose.

"My name is Masefield," he said, coming in and shutting the door behind him, looking around, taking the place in at a glance.

"I dough."

"And you must be Buster."

"Yeah, I'm Buster." I went to the fridge and got some apple juice. So he knew about me. That was good. That was something. Not much. I felt thoroughly depressed by his appearance. Plus, going into shock. "Want some juice?"

"No thanks. You sound like you've got a terrible cold."

"I do. Sunny's at the post office. It's where she works."

We looked at each other. Then he looked out at the bay. "It's all just as I imagined it," he said. "From Sunny's letters. I almost expect to see her mom out there in her one-design."

"How long are you here for?"

"I don't know. I promised Sunny I'd come."

"That was five years ago."

"I've been in prison. In Russia."

I completely despaired. If it had been any reason but that, I'd have run him out of town. But what can you do with a reason of that magnitude? The guy was in prison in Russia, for Pete's sake, probably Siberia. I thought of how incredibly happy I'd been the last five years, and here this poor guy was moldering away in some cell or camp. "That's awful," I said despairingly. "It's horrible." I clasped my brow, thinking, Oh, God! God!

There was nothing I could do or say in the face of such an appalling fact as Masefield in Siberia. I remembered my vow. I remembered that loving someone was putting their happiness before your own.

"Look... uh, Masefield, I'm going away for a while. I'm going away so you can have your visit with Sunny." I looked around, wondering what to take. I grabbed my pack and just started throwing stuff into it. In a way, I didn't know what I was doing. I felt like I was going crazy. "I told her once that when you came I'd go. So that's what I'm doing." I just threw stuff in, stuff of little M's and Sunny's along with mine, anything that came to hand. I only had one thing on my mind and that was to get out. Fast. To go.

Masefield watched. The guy was in complete control, the opposite of me. He looked like he didn't know what it was to lose control. The complete opposite of me. I suppose you learn it in prison. He looked like Abraham Lincoln or someone like that.

"Look, stay here for a few minutes, okay? Don't go to the post office for about ten minutes. Give me time to get away."

I pulled on my jeans over my sweatpants. Heck, I wasn't going to show him my cock. I pulled on the pack, then took it off again to put on my shirt and jacket first. Then I was off, out the door, running down the pier. Before I left town, I had to say good-bye to M. Sunny would understand, but he wouldn't. I didn't want to seem to desert him. God, I wished I could take him with me. And Sunny too. How could I live without them, even for a day?

I burst into the day school like a wild man. "I've got to talk to M," I told the teacher. M came running over to me and I took him into another room. We both sat on those tiny little chairs they have in nursery schools. I leaned toward him. My pack felt huge on my back. God knows what was in it. "I've got to go away, M, sweetheart. It's just for a while and I *promise* I'll be back."

"Go away?"

"Just listen. Don't talk." I felt incredibly pressed for time. I felt I had to get out of town in minutes or else...

Or else I'd see them together.

"M, I love you with all my heart. You know that. Don't ever forget it."

God, I'd seen him every day since he was born. Every day.

"Are you going looking for someone?"

"No, it's just a trip. I'm going on a trip. I'll write to you. I'll send you postcards, okay? So you'll always know where I am. I'll call, too, on the telephone."

"Are you going to be hiding out?"

"No." I could see he didn't understand. He didn't have any concept of my going somewhere, of my not being here, a part of his life. I didn't, either.

"Good-bye, M." I hugged him and kissed him. "I love you and I love your mom. Forever. I promise."

I got up from the tiny chair and ran out the door. He started running after me, calling, "Buster! Buster!"

"Oh, God. Oh, God." I jumped on my bike and started pedaling through town as fast as I could. It was horrible. I knew he was still chasing me and he was a really fast runner for such a little kid. I could hear him calling. People were coming out on the street. Oh, God, there was Sunny, stepping out of the P.O. "Buster," she called out. "What on earth!"

"Catch him," I shouted to her like a maniac, feeling so desperate. "Stop him. Tell him I'll be back."

"Buster, why do you have a pack? Stop! You're sick in bed! Stop him," she shouted, to the townspeople, "he's got a cold!"

Instead of stopping little M, she started running after me, too, shouting, "Buster, stop!"

Along with Sunny's voice I could hear M's little voice calling, "Daddy, Daddy!"

# 21. THE WIND

I couldn't believe my eyes when I looked out the P.O. window and saw Buster, who I'd left sick in bed babying himself to death, pedaling like a maniac out of town. He was hunched over the handlebars, his eyes bulging out, and looked like a man pursued by demons. He had a gigantic pack on his back with stuff spilling out of it.

It scared me. I ran out of the P.O. and there was little M running after him with all his might. And, way behind M, on chubby legs, ran Laurie. What on earth was going on? I started shouting at Buster and then joined the parade, running after M, who was running after Buster with his little arms and fingers whirling like windmills.

After about half a mile of this it was clear that Buster, now a speck in the distance, wasn't going to stop, plus it was against the law for me to abandon my post office. Even so, I had a struggle convincing M to stop running and turn around and walk back with me.

"He said he was going on a trip. What's a trip?" M beseeched me. "Besides falling down, I mean? When will he be back? He said he loves us but why would he come to school to tell me he loves us and then run away? Did he go away because of his cold? Is this what dying is?"

Those were just a few of the questions little M asked me on our walk back. I tried to answer him but my mind was numb. It didn't make any sense at all.

Pretty soon we came upon Laurie, red-faced, stumbling, crying. "You left me," she accused M. "You ran away without telling me."

We were all so afraid of losing each other.

And then, as we drew abreast of the market I saw a tall lean figure walking into town from the other direction, from my water house, which was a half mile the other way, and then I understood everything. Masefield had come. I knew he hadn't seen me yet, having normal eyesight, so luckily I could prepare.

Quickly I turned up the side street and put M and Laurie back in school. Then I ran into the restaurant and told Chris, "He's come." She was carrying a tray of dirty breakfast dishes at the time and had to set them down.

"Oh!" She turned pale, knowing at once who I meant. I'd told her about the letter I got last month but did not tell Buster, since I wasn't at all sure it meant anything and didn't want to disturb him. "After school, take M home with you and Laurie, okay?"

"Sure. Of course!"

Then back to the street again and by now Masefield was almost to the P.O., my abandoned post. He looked stunning. He looked so different from anyone around here, he could have been from another planet. My heart was thumping away, but I determined to be cool. I just walked toward him, didn't run. "Hey, Masefield!"

He saw me and slowly smiled. "Sunny!"

"Masefield!"

We came together so fast that maybe I did run after all. Maybe he did too. I think he did. "You've come!" I threw myself into his arms and he held me with all his might. "You've come!"

"Didn't I say I would?"

"I never stopped waiting. Not once."

"Me too. I waited and waited to come."

What is a trip? little M asked me. I could have responded, A trip is like a visit. A trip is going away for a while and a visit is coming to stay for a while. The visitor is also on a trip.

It became clear to me at once that Masefield was just here on a visit. He hadn't come to stay with me, to be with me, to remain with me.

What wasn't clear was how long his visit would last. A day, a month, a year? I could have asked but I didn't want to know.

I thought of Buster. That first night when I lay with Masefield was a torment because I thought so much about Buster. Masefield's thinness after Buster's giant burliness, seemed to cut my skin like a knife. And there was no warmth to the man. Something had died in him in prison. The light was gone from his eyes and soul—the youth and the eagerness. I knew it was up to me to bring him to life, to replenish him, and that's why he'd come.

I thought of Buster when I told Masefield he had a little son, named after him because, even as I told him I knew, then and finally, that it wasn't true, only factual. Buster and M knew the real truth of it.

Mostly I thought of Buster when I woke in the night. A wind had come up and was sobbing through the trees and over the water, and it seemed to me it was Buster sobbing his heart out in the night outside the door, knowing I was lying with Masefield. I even slipped quietly out of bed to go to the door to see if he was there. He wasn't. It was the wind. But I knew that wherever he had thrown down his bag that night he was thinking of me being with Masefield and crying aloud, sopping the ground with tears and snot that just kept producing and reproducing, gasping for breath, turning the ground around him into a tear-marsh, a snot-bog.

Even so I made love to Masefield like a woman starved for love. It was as if I'd been the one imprisoned all the years.

I kissed every inch of his body. I sucked his cock like a starved babe going for mother's milk. I put his cock inside me again, and again, even when he was too soft to enter, I stuffed him in and made him grow inside me or came on his softness, not caring. Or he put his tongue hard against me and I came and came. I wanted to imprint my body on his, his on mine. I wanted to not know whose body was whose, have it not matter, be one.

Although I'd told him in Paris I would go on with my life while I waited, I hadn't. Life had gone on—it always will —but I hadn't lived it, or if I had, it was a half-life. Waiting is not living. Being without the person you love is not living. I'd gone through the motions. I never wanted to live like that again.

All I could think now was that when Masefield left, when his visit was over, I would die.

This realization freed me. Now I would not be anxious about when or how soon he'd go. Now I would not dread being left here without him, having to resume the half-life, loving Buster and M with half a love, haunted by my mother on the bay, and badgered by the insane Bart Blainey on the roads.

Maybe Masefield could put his investigative powers to work for me while he was here, finding Mom and finding out where Daddy was. Then I could say good-bye to them before doing away with myself. It would be my turn to leave them. Only I would wholly leave, not half leave as they did me, as Masefield would do to me, too.

Yes, finally I could *do* something. I could act instead of wait and look and yearn and hope.

And M would be okay, would still have a mother and father, Chris and Buster, so he would be all right. And Masefield would have the world he cared so much about, the world he loved more than he did me and always would.

Meanwhile, freed by my decision, I would love him unreservedly—and joyfully, too, once the wind died down and I stopped hearing Buster cry.

Now it was almost dawn. I thought Masefield was asleep, but he spoke. "Hemingway died," he said.

"Oh, no! I didn't realize. How sad."

"In the summer. July. While I was staying with the count, I caught up with all that had happened in the world these last years, and that was one of the worst things. He shot himself. Put a rifle in his mouth and blew his brains out."

"Why?"

"I don't know."

I remembered sitting at the Deux Magots. It seemed a million years ago. But here was Masefield with me now in Inverness. "He said I'd find Mom, remember?"

"Yes. You did, too."

Masefield looked so grave. He looked like he'd forgotten the meaning of the word smile. Here we were, truly so happy to have reunited but so sad too, talking of death and suicide.

Maybe it is when you are feeling most intensely alive that you are most intensely aware of death, the flip side. An orgasm is a little death in itself and we'd had a number of them. Our hearts had stopped.

"Yes, I found Mom, but not to have, not to keep."

"You can't *have* people, Sunny. You can't keep them."

I thought about that and said, "No, but . . . you can find them so as to be with them. When you love somebody you want to be with them. Loving a person is wanting to be with that person. Being—"

"All right, all right. I get it."

I think Masefield didn't like repetition as much as he used to.

"Masefield, do you think Hemingway killed himself because he couldn't be with someone?"

"No."

"I don't, either. But people do."

"Yes, but it's not a good reason."

I wanted to ask him what he would consider a good reason but decided not to. When a person has been in prison for four years it's hard not to feel that everything you say to them is highly superficial. Especially when talking about something I'd just thought about for the first time and that he'd probably thought about a lot.

Here we were talking about death. In Paris we'd chattered and giggled and he'd shown me his tongue trick. We'd talked about ourselves, our lives. Now we didn't need to because, strangely, this distance of almost five years seemed ultimately to have drawn us closer. On a deep level we knew each other, appreciated that we'd each been through different kinds of hell during which the image of each other, the love, had supported us, kept us sane and surviving. It was as if we'd been through it together.

Masefield was still thinking about Hemingway. "Whatever

reason someone has for suiciding must seem like a good reason to them at the time."

Buster had wanted to kill himself when I told him about Masefield. Chris had wanted to when she found out she was pregnant. But both of them were still alive. Maybe I would still be alive too.

Time will tell, as Daddy, outstandingly vague, used to say.

Masefield, tuned into my thoughts, now asked, "Where do you think your dad is now?"

"God knows."

"All the craziness started when we were together in Paris. Maybe it will all end now that we're back together."

"That's what I've been thinking too. I hope so."

"Time will tell," said Masefield. "It always does."

Masefield and Daddy knew something about time that I didn't know. Buster, too, because he told me once, "If I had killed myself that night, I never would have found out what happened," and when I looked blank, he explained, "To us, to our lives."

"But if you'd died, it wouldn't have happened."

"Well, some of it would have. Little M would have been born, but I wouldn't have got to be there. I'm glad I lived through the pain of that night of learning about you and Masefield so I could have these wonderful years with you and M."

As I drifted off to sleep, I hoped with all my heart that, wherever he was, he was living through the worse pain of this night and would in time be glad he'd lived. I hoped there were many more years of happiness in store for Buster because he was the best of the best.

If only . . . oh, if only his happiness didn't depend on me.

Later, waking again to the wailing of the wind, I had to go once more to the door . . . to be sure.

## 22. HAVING BEEN A DIARY

This evening at eleven o'clock, looking north across the bay to Nova Scotia, I saw a stupendous display of northern lights. It changed the night, streaking and flashing across the sky, now rosy pink, then fading away to white shafts of brilliant light. Its period of greatest brilliancy lasted about fifteen minutes and then slowly dimmed and disappeared. It is unusual to see such a sight in this latitude, although I remember seeing them in Boston when I was young. Being here in Gloucester in this shack overlooking Ipswich Bay that I built with Pa forty years ago is bringing back memories of my youth to me, continuing and aiding the investigation of my lost emotions begun when I left Inverness. Probably I should have come here first of all, should have begun here in this cottage my odyssey of personal rediscovery. But I was too hungry to see the world that had been denied me since the death of Andy and the madness of his mother.

I am quite snug. The Franklin stove still works. I have built pine shelves and my boxes of books that have tagged around after me all these years have come home to this cottage to roost. At night I sit before the fire, having split wood during the day, and take from the shelves some excellent mind to spend the evening with, to engage with. It's a marvel to me how many smart men have walked the earth and were considerate enough to leave us a message. I wonder if Andy would have been of their number. I believe so. After my reading, I climb the ladder to the loft and sleep under the eaves, lulled by the sound of seawater kissing the continent. During the day, I sit on the porch and look at the ocean, or go down to the rocks and look at it even closer.

I think I will get a dory so I can row out and catch some fish.

I still don't write, but I have stopped drinking and crying. I use my body and my hands and they complain about it but meanwhile tremblingly come to life. When I am lonely I walk to the village and find someone to pass the time of day with, or I take down a book. Loneliness is all right as long as it is calm, not desperate. I am calm.

During the cleanup of the cottage, after thirty years of neglect, I found a journal I had written my first year of college, where I had gone on scholarship, as a country bumpkin, a farm boy, age fourteen.

On the khaki-colored cover of the notebook was my name, Muir Scott, Cambridge, Mass., under which was the title "Being a Diary." "Being" was crossed out and changed to "Having Been."

"Monday, October 1, 1917. I am going to write down from day to day all that I do in Harvard. This begins my second week here. I spent Saturday and Sunday home at the farm. Pa and I dug potatoes. I also harvested my peanuts. There was about a quart of full-grown ones.

"Tuesday, October 2. This morning before my English recitation, I went over and walked around the stadium. On the way back on the other side of the street, I noticed a thriving truck garden which the frost had not yet injured. There was not a weed in it and the rows were so straight that it was a pleasure to look at.

"I studied Spanish until lunchtime and after lunch went for a walk up Garden Street to visit the Harvard Botanic Garden. I was interested in the greenhouse plants which were entirely new to me. Some had sweet-smelling odors which attracted the bees; others had brilliant, complicated flowers rising up in a single spike, and others had pendulous cups—for catching insects, I suppose.

"I spent an hour and a half wandering around and then started off for the Charles River intending to walk home along its banks. The Charles is not a very wide river, not nearly as wide as the Merrimack, but it is infinitely more winding, making horse-shoe curves in some places. Also, while the Merrimack is muddy and dirty from the sewage of half a dozen large cities, the Charles seems to be clean and pure—in comparison, anyway.

"Some of the oarsmen were out rowing in light skiffs for prac-tice. A little farther down were three snow-white swans, the first that I have ever seen. They seemed to expect something from me so tomorrow I am going to save a slice of bread from lunch and give it to them if I can find them. Now I'll have to study my French before bedtime.

"Thursday, Oct. 4. Received from ma $.50. Spent: carfare $.05, paper $.01. Yesterday I went to feed the swans and when I got back I found a telephone message from pa to come home if I could do so. Thinking that the house had burned down or something, I grabbed a suitcase and beat it for the subway and train. When I got home I found that ma had felt sure that I would come so in order not to disappoint her he called me up!

"I got back here at midnight and this morning nearly over-slept. Still I took the oral exams in German today and passed. . . ."

Ah-ha! I thought. A clue. Fifty miles of travel going to Lawrence and returning, hours spent on subway and train so as not to *disappoint* ma. But the only expression of my incredible staggering anger was that little exclamation point. It wasn't enough that I went home every weekend to work on the farm, but I had to rush down on a Wednesday because she had *felt sure* I would come.

Yes, there are stirrings of memory, as if my brain were wrin-kling its brow. Something happened that freshman year between me and ma, something awful.

• • •

"Monday, Oct. 8. Spent: movies $.20, paper $.01, carfare $.10, watch repair $.25. I had lab in physics this morning, then took the oral exam in French and it was about the easiest thing I ever struck. Sunday pa and I went over to the farm and dug potatoes and pulled beans. He is going to shell a few every night. I hope we will have some baked next Saturday night.

"Tuesday, October 9. After a long deliberation I bought a fountain pen. I didn't want to be extravagant, but I really need a fountain pen as all work in class should be written in ink. It would be rather inconvenient to carry a bottle of ink around with me. Besides, I have wanted one for a long time and I already look upon it as a lifelong friend in the same way as I do my watch. I hope I won't lose it or break it. Just the same, I'm scared that ma will think I hadn't ought to have spent the money for it.

"Friday, October 12. Spent: books $.80, $.35, $.85; stamps $.05, $.50 watch repair. Yesterday the Shermans came over. They are going to call their new baby Elizabeth, which is about the worst name I can think of. Everyone will call her Lizzy. It's awful to wish a name like that onto anyone. The kid has my sincere sympathy.

"I have some narcissus bulbs started in a dish. They ought to blossom before Christmas.

"I got an awful surprise today. Ma has actually gone to work at the harness shop! She earned $1.15 the first day and hopes to earn $2.00 a day soon."

Had ma gone to work in the harness shop to help pay for my lifelong friend the fountain pen? Probably. But I did need it for my work, and at least it wasn't going to be breaking all the time like my good friend the watch, according to all the monies spent for repair. I'm suspicious about those watch repair amounts.

"Wednesday, Oct. 31. The Italians seem to be retreating before the Germans and Austrians. Let's hope they'll stiffen up soon. Our soldiers have been on the front for 2 or 3 days. They are going to send the shell case of the first shot fired to President Wilson.

"Tuesday, Nov. 6. Spent: postcards $.03, stamps $.02, carfare $.10, $.75 watch repair. Ma picked out a suit for me last Sunday and of course I said it was all right.

"I bought a pretty little plant yesterday with pink blossoms. It looks like a kind of begonia."

When had I stopped growing flowers? Why, it was after Andy died. I just couldn't stand to go into the garden because he'd always worked with me there—it was our special time together every day—and it was just too unbearable to bend over the flowers and remember his voice asking about them, remember how he'd worked so valiantly by my side: weeding and watering, planting and pruning, how he took such an interest in every aspect of it.

When I deserted the garden, his mom took it over rather than let it die, and she did pretty well too, considering she was so uninclined.

But what a deprivation I laid on myself, giving up that garden, constituting a double loss for myself: Andy and the flowers.

And never grieving, never grieving.

I stopped looking for references to ma in the diary and instead looked for entries about flowers, growing astounded at how numerous they were.

"I have a crocus bulb that has blossomed out. It is purple with delicate darker stripes at the base. It closes up whenever the room gets cold so I don't need a thermometer. I have also a tulip and a hyacinth. I'm pretty sure the latter will blossom."

"I went for a walk after math and saw an English primrose in a florist's shop. It was such a beautiful thing and looked so cheery that I couldn't help buying it. It looks great in the room alongside my hyacinth, which has blossomed out and it smells so nice that I guess I'll wear it out smelling it."

· · ·

"I wish I had some sort of dish for my Japanese lily. The pot it's in isn't right and it's all rotting away. I'll have to try to get something in Boston."

I wonder if the garden in Inverness is dead. Why, of course it is. Sunny doesn't even live there anymore. Poor Sunny, why couldn't we have loved her? I tried to love her to make up for her mother not. I gave her what mother love I could, my father love having been all spent on Andy and dying with him.

I never thanked his mom for providing me with flowers, for filling every room every day with flowers. She knew how I loved and needed them and knew I could no longer go to the garden. She provided me that service although she was completely disinclined, and I don't believe I ever expressed my thanks.

It has been five years now since I went away. That's a long time. It's probably been over a year since I last called Sunny. I have a little grandson I don't know, will never see.

Ma in the harness shop, me buying flowers.

My brain cast about fervently for the elusive memory. I began to get a frightful headache. I believe it was something about flowers, that terrible thing that happened between me and ma. But what?

She began to go crazy again. I just couldn't stand it even one more time. I'd come to the end of my tether. She got that look on her face that I'd come to dread, the eyes looking inward, the face expressing not so much sorrow as fear, anxiety. And she put on the same outfit every time she went crazy, the same outfit that I'd tried once to burn and another time to bury. . . .

No, no, that was Mom going looking for Andy, not ma. Ma never went crazy or happy or sad or silly. She just got disappointed. Although I was a good boy, helpful and smart, I always managed to let her down.

Something happened. I wanted to kill her. I didn't kill her but I wanted to and she knew that I did.

Had she made a surprise visit to Cambridge to see her young paragon of industry in room B33, James Smith Hall, and found him surrounded by flowers of every size and description, lolling amidst masses of blooms of every hue, in a room heady with scents, perhaps busy with bees and butterflies as well, a veritable hothouse, my own little botanical heaven in the middle of the winter?

No, no, she never came to my room. Nor did Pa. He came down to Boston and I always met him there walking across the bridge from Cambridge to do so, for I was always walking everywhere, the better to mask my flower expenses under carfare, not to mention under watch repair.

No, I can't remember what happened with me and ma. I'll never know. And yet, and yet, a vision comes to me now of breaking dishes. I wanted to kill her but instead I broke her dishes, all of the china dishes we'd used for supper that night.

(What night?)

I smashed them one by one at her feet, shouting, "Yes! A dish! Yes, I did! A dish!"

What on earth?

What dish? Could it have been . . . yes! Yes, it was the dish for the rotting Japanese lily!

One day I'd gone to Boston to meet Pa and, passing a store window, saw the perfect dish and bought it. Pa, seeing the package in my pocket, asked me what it was I had and I must have told him a dish but not what it was for.

Then, home the next weekend, very tired from midterms, from farmwork, and also from the housework she always expected me to do as well, it was while washing the dishes, Sunday night, with the train still to catch back to Boston, that I was questioned about the mystery dish by ma. She was sitting at the kitchen table interrogating me minutely as she always did about my life, studies, work, expenses.

Finally she inquired about the dish that Pa had discovered on my person in Boston. I held out for the longest time, all through the washing of the dishes. I refused to say a word about it, dared to grow stubborn and protect my secret garden.

But she was a skilled inquisitor and she broke me down. She made me tell. And then, having heard the awful truth, she said with trembling voice, toned high with disbelief, tears of disappointment and hurt brimming in her eyes, "A dish for a lily? You paid money for a lily and then you went to Boston and bought a dish for it? Because it was rotting? A *dish for a rotting lily?*"

"Yes!" Crash! "A dish!" Crash! "I did!" Crash!

I laid down the diary, my head splitting, my body pouring sweat.

So, it would seem that I wanted to kill my mother over a dish for a rotting lily.

But from here I can see the sensitive and exhausted child prodigy in a room of posies that asked nothing of the boy, only gave him the pleasure of their sight and scent, the pleasure of letting him care for them and love them and learn from them.

And from here I can see the mother who could not understand, who wanted so much from her son, more than he could give, especially what she most wanted, love, love that, incomprehensibly to her, he had showered on a rotting lily. He'd broken her heart.

She had a stroke that night, became bedridden, lingered a year or so, and died.

He (I) had put the dish drainer on the floor with the broken pieces of china so that it would look like I'd dropped them when she had her seizure. Then I called the doctor.

And what about the mother of my children? I think it was the outfit, her going to get the same old outfit to put on so as to turn the clock back and have it be the day that Andy died. Or, who knows, maybe it was just the look on her face, the eyes turning inward, the fear.

Yes? What about it? What then? Did I do something else that I've forgotten in the same way that I forgot this incident of forty-four years ago? Am I going to have to go back to Inverness and find out what, if anything, it was?

I looked about at my snug cabin, my haven where at last I'd found peace in the form of calm loneliness. I did not want to go back.

Say I don't have to go back.

Whom was I asking? God? Since there is no God, I must be asking me. There's no one else around. I could be asking all the smart men stacked up around me in resinous shelves, but they'd all have different answers. It must be me. What, then, will I answer? Must I return to Inverness?

No, I replied somewhat smugly.

Of course that is your answer, I said irritably to myself. Because you are willing, in this investigation of your true self, to discover capabilities of grief but not of unkindness, not of cruelty.

At this I felt so chastened that my inquisitor self took a kinder tone (maybe it *was* God): Will you not face honestly this discovery you have just wracked your brain to make? Will you not now, at last, look into your soul?

I did not mean to hurt my mother.

## 23. THE ALBATROSS

I woke up with Sunny still sleeping in my arms. The hills across the bay had turned green from the winter rains and were alight in the morning mist, almost blinding in their emeraldness. When I'd arrived in Inverness they'd been gold. Three months ago. Three months! I couldn't believe I'd been here so long. It was as if I were under a spell. The place had thrown an enchanted spell over me. I had no sense of time passing. I felt like tomorrow I could wake up and the hills would be gold again. And I was so cut off from the world I might as well still be in prison. The only radio stations you could get out here didn't have classical music, and opera was anathema. You couldn't get the *New York Times*, and the San Francisco papers were written on a third-grade level by grammer school dropouts. I'd exhausted the tiny lending library, and although my one foray to San Francisco for some of the new titles—*Franny and Zooey, Catch 22, Nobody Knows My Name*—was a success, I despaired to see how unhappy Sunny was to be in a city. It wasn't just the city, it was being away from Inverness, where she might miss catching a glimpse of her mother on the bay. She was still completely possessed. I would have to do something about it, I don't know what. I realized she was never out of sight of the bay from her home or P.O., and whatever she may be doing, be it washing dishes or canceling letters, she's simultaneously scanning the waters for her mom. Only at night did she relax her vigil.

I had a letter from Washington to report back. Rest and rehabilitation time was up. When had the letter come? Weeks ago. I didn't even know where it was. I was rested. Rehabilitated too. Restored to good health and the ability to work, the ability to spy, the ability, if necessary, to steal and kill. If I stayed here much longer, I would lose those abilities just restored to me all unknowingly by Sunny's loving care because the edge that has returned to me would grow dull and blurred from being in this dream world.

Poor Sunny, to spend these months caring for me, only to enable me to leave her. She'd never once asked me if I would go, when I would go. But she knows I will.

And I can't take her. There's no place to take her to, even if she'd come. I could marry her, but would that be fair? She would have to live in ignorance of my work and whereabouts, would see me rarely. Better she make a life for herself here. With Buster. She misses Buster terribly. More than she knows. That first night we were together she must have gone to the door ten times thinking he was there.

Buster pedaled east out of town, out of state, and now had pedaled himself across the entire nation to the eastern seaboard, where he found himself stalled from further pedaling by an ocean.

Periodically he called M at Chris's house, where, since the day of my arrival in November, the kid still stayed. Sunny hung on every word from M of Buster's progress across the country, as did I. The man was a mountain of strength and endurance. It wouldn't surprise me if he became the first man to pedal around the world.

Sunny's hair was aglow with the same morning light that illuminated the hills and it shone like the shining bay. Her hair was so straight and sleek that even after a night's sleep it never got a snarl. I could run my fingers through it and it would fall back into place exactly. Sunny actually had no color to her hair or her eyes, and yet she was full of light. She *was* light. She'd been my beacon since I'd met her in Paris and always would be. I'd always come back to her. If I was ever able to get *away* from her, that is. But was that fair to always come back and butt into her life with Buster?

Anyway, I won't worry about coming back to Sunny until I've worried about getting away. I can't even get up to get the morning paper, let alone leave town. I'd better at least answer the letter to the service. Today. After we go for our sail. I wonder if there's any way to mail a letter in this town without Sunny seeing it?

I wonder if there's any way to ease out of bed without waking Sunny and having to make love?

I'd set a formidable precedent with Sunny that first night in Paris. The woman seemed to think I had supernatural powers, and I must say that with her I felt like I did. No, not felt like I did, did. She herself seemed to be in a constant state of arousal. Usually with a woman, you satisfy your desire and days go by before desire for her returns, if ever. But with Sunny, a little made you want more and more made you want tons.

Now I had a hard-on from just thinking about it. Maybe I'd surprise her and just slip it in while she was asleep. Two bits says she's ready for me in her sleep, wet and juicy and ready for the giant cock. Yes, just as I thought. The woman's amazing.

I turned her toward me so she wouldn't simultaneously be looking for Mom.

"Where's Mom?" M walked in just as I was coming out of the shower.

"She went to the village for supplies. Then she's going to sail from the yacht club and pick us up here. We'll sail over to Heart's Desire Beach, anchor, and picnic. How does that sound?"

"Fine."

M and I had a guarded relationship, polite and unaffectionate. There was no hostility, no real hatred or aversion, but a definite sense of mutual mistrust and general lack of appreciation for each other's charms.

The kid was no fool. He could put two and two together. His

beloved Buster had gone because I had come. Ergo, I was a villain.

Naturally, even though I understood his feelings, I was highly resentful that he wouldn't even give me a chance.

Sunny had meant to do what she felt was the right thing by telling M from day one that I was his real father and explaining how that came to be, but it had ricocheted and he'd say things like "Buster's my daddy and you're my sperm."

"That's great," I'd say bitterly. "Just great. Thanks, pal."

"Just what I always wanted to be," I'd tell Sunny, "somebody's sperm."

"Oh, give him a chance," she'd say, laughing. "He'll come round."

"Me give *him* a chance!"

One thing I had going for me was the Indian magic I learned from Count Von Luckner. It really wowed him that I could make things appear and disappear. But you don't want mystery to become commonplace, so I'd rarely perform and this would, in the long run, gripe him.

"Why won't you do the magic more if it pleases him so much?" would ask his mother.

"I'm his father, not a performing monkey."

I also could please him by telling stories—thanks again to the count, who had so many good ones, I being one of those people who can't make stories out of his life.

Naturally Buster, to hear M tell it, had only to go to town for milk to come back with a ripsnorting tale of real-life adventure.

This day, while waiting for Sunny, I told him about the count and the albatross.

"He was only fourteen years old when he ran away from home and went sailing before the mast."

"Like we're going to do today?"

We were sitting on the water house deck, our legs dangling off the edge, waiting for Sunny to sail by and pick us up.

"Sort of."

"I'm only four going on five. Fourteen's pretty grown up, actually."

Was the kid trying to annoy me, or was this how kids were?

"But M," I said patiently. "This was on a huge three-masted clipper ship with about thirty sails, and instead of going around a bay it went around the whole world."

"Oh."

"And he left home for years, not for the afternoon. It was not an afternoon sail with his mother and father."

"Buster's my real—"

"Look, do you want to hear the story or not?"

"Okay."

"Good. Well, on this big sailing ship, they kept pigs in the hold below, I forget why, maybe they were delivering them somewhere, and it was the count's job to clean out their stalls and feed them.

"It was the lowliest job on the whole ship and he was the lowliest person. Nobody knew he was really a count.

"So one day, when he was climbing the mast, just for fun and to see if he could do it, he lost his footing and fell overboard, and because he was just the lowly pigkeeper, the captain didn't think it was important to try to save him.

"There were some other men on the boat who thought he was a good kid and they wanted to save him just because they liked him. But while they were arguing about it with the captain, the ship was getting farther and farther away from the count because with all those sails on they could go pretty fast, and the trouble was, with a rough sea like that was, if they got too far away, they wouldn't be able to see him anymore.

"So there's the count, just a kid, in the middle of the huge ocean . . ."

"In the middle of the whole world he was going around," M added.

"Right, and he was swimming after the ship like crazy and he was a strong swimmer, but that ship was going so much faster than he was that it was hopeless, even though by then the good guys on the ship had lowered a boat and were going to try and save him."

I had his interest. He was all attention.

"Now, M, there is a big, beautiful white sea bird called an albatross. They're four feet long, which is about as long as you, and they have a wing spread of twelve feet, which would be as long as two of me.

"This albatross bird came swooping down, curious to see what thing this was swimming on the water because it didn't look like a seal or a fish or a dolphin or any kind of bird of his acquaintance. He flew down to get a look at the thing's face, and when he was right above the count's head, the count reached up and grabbed hold of its feet. This accomplished two wonderful things. It kept him afloat because he was getting too tired to swim anymore, and it showed the men in the boat where he was because the albatross, trying to fly away, kept beating his huge white wings, which the men could see above the waves that were hiding the count."

"Was it hard for him to hold on?"

"Very hard. Because the terrible thing was that the albatross began to peck at the count's hands to make him let go, and boy, did that hurt. In his whole life he'd never felt anything so painful, but he didn't dare to let go because he knew he'd drown if he did.

"The bird pecked his hands right down to the bone and he was streaming with blood, but the men steered the boat for the big flapping bird and saved him."

"Gee. That's a neat story."

M was quiet a while, then he turned to me and asked quite charmingly, "Will you show me an albatross?"

"I'd be glad to, but they don't live in this part of the world."

"I mean magic me up one." M pointed to the bay as if to say, See, you have the proper backdrop, it's not as if we're in a living room where the big bird couldn't fly without knocking over the lamps.

To create a successful illusion, I needed something to start with—a gull or even a land bird—but the bay was strangely empty except for a man in a dory. "I can't now, M, because here comes your mom," and, so saying, I turned the dory man into Sunny tacking toward us. M stood up, waving, and just when it looked like she was going to sail right into the deck so that M was grabbing hold of me with fear, she disappeared. M's face was a study, his eyes like dishes. Then he turned to me and burst out laughing.

"You did Mom!" he said.

"Yeah, I did."

He looked at me with genuine admiration. "Wow!"

As I was sitting and he was standing, he even gave me a little hug because of his excitement and pleasure. It was nice. I wouldn't be anywhere with this kid if it weren't for the count.

A few minutes later, watching Sunny really come tacking toward us, I said to M, "Do you know what else about that albatross story?"

"What?"

"Well, the count became a famous sea captain and a great man, but even to this day, *sixty five years later*, when he tells that story, his hands start to shake and tremble from remembering that albatross pecking at them."

M looked very thoughtful. "Buster's whole body trembles when he thinks about going into the water. Does that mean something bad happened to him one time in water when he was little?"

"Why, yes, I'd say that it did. I'd say something really bad happened."

"As bad as what happened to the count's hands?"

"Yes."

"Maybe something pecked at his whole body. Poor Buster."

"Poor Buster," I agreed, feeling generous toward Buster (God knows he'd been generous to me) and meaning it, too, because of feeling this fine new companionship with M . . . with my son.

M had told me before about Buster's fear of water, but like anything he said about Buster, he made it sound like something to admire, made me feel I was lacking in feeling because I *wasn't* afraid of the water, but this time I put it together with other stuff I'd learned about Buster, and the absolutely staggering thought hit me that Buster could be Andy.

# 24. SAILING TOWARD
# MY MASEFIELDS

There the two of them were, sitting on the deck, waving at me and looking, for once, rather at ease and happy together.

It was a shame that they were so difficult with each other. I'd been able to prepare M somewhat for Masefield coming home one day, but I hadn't been able to prepare Masefield at all for a young son being here when he at last came. It was a big adjustment for them both.

I'd say to M, "Honey, you're not being disloyal to Buster if you allow yourself to like Masefield," and he would look at me as if to say, "That may be the way you operate but not me," and I would say, trying to explain Masefield's lack of attention, "Masefield didn't even know you were alive."

"Then how come he put the sperm in you and made me?"

"Sometimes I wish I'd never told that sperm story. I just tried to do the right thing by everyone and live honestly. . . ."

"It was Buster who birthed me."

"But that doesn't make a person your daddy," I said exasperatedly. "Most women have a doctor birth the baby like Chris did with Laurie, and the doctor doesn't then become the baby's father, for God's sake, just because he happened to officiate at the birth!"

"Who is Laurie's daddy, by the way?"

"Never mind. We're talking about us."

"Laurie thinks you're her mother, too—as well as mine."

"I am. In the way that Buster's your father . . . too."

This was typical of the tangled type of conversation M and I were wont to have.

"Well, I just know that Buster's the one who's been my daddy the whole time." At this, M burst into tears.

"I know he has, M," I said, putting my arms around him. His body felt so tiny and tight. "He has been your daddy, and he loves you with all his heart."

"I want him to come home," M bawled.

"He will come home," I promised in a quavery voice, feeling all weepy myself, "but in the meantime, couldn't you just try to love Masefield?"

"No. I hate him."

Luckily Chris had kept M with her and Laurie because Masefield and I had a lot of adjusting to do about each other, too. Deep down we knew and loved each other, but on top we were strangers.

These three months with Masefield had not been easy. Compared to my harmonious life with Buster, where there was never a cross word, it was very, well, "lively" would be a nice word to describe our relationship.

What it came down to was that two weeks in Paris five years ago hardly could constitute an intimate understanding even though it had set in motion a child and a seemingly deathless passion.

We were different. Boy, were we different.

Countless times we had stood in rigid fury in separate corners of the room knowing we had only to touch each other for all to be forgiven. Our bodies understood each other; our very cells were compatible even if our personalities weren't.

I hated his smoking, which was obnoxious as well as making his tongue taste bitter.

He hated the fact that although I tried to play chess I never got any better and would get mad and tip over the board when he took my queen.

I hated the fact that he read about five hours a day, he that I didn't read at all.

I really did read some, but he considered it not at all and we fought about how much I actually did read. It's true I *pretended* to read some of the time and then he accused me, rightly, of really looking out at the bay the whole time. Whereupon I said that I *thought* about things, that reading wasn't thinking as much as thinking was and he turned around and said I wasn't thinking, I was looking at the bay. "For Mom!" he would add, sometimes shouting.

One thing he had grown more and more unable to tolerate was my looking for Mom. Actually I wasn't looking for her half as much as he thought I was. It's impossible to live smack out on the bay as we did and not look at it the majority of the time. However, glancing at the bay as I, granted, often do is not looking for Mom. I am looking at an egret or a boat or the hills on the other side. I am looking at a cloud or the moon rising or a rainbow. But try to tell Masefield that.

As well, we both thought the other one was too sexually demanding and that our relationship was too sustained by sex, which it was, but what was wrong with that? I think we were lucky to feel so sexy about each other and lucky that our sex was so heaven sent, but he said we should have other things going too.

"Like chess and reading, I suppose?" I said bitterly.

"Right. Or if you at least liked music!" he beseeched me. "If we could listen to Mozart together!" he'd cry out with what seemed like true anguish.

"But whenever I suggest we do something else like go for a sail or a walk," I reminded him indignantly, "you're the one that wants to go to bed!"

"Because it beats the hell out of sailing."

"But not reading?" I'd say incredulously. "You'd rather read than make love? You're crazy. Although, come to think of it, I'd much rather sail than have sex. If I had to do without one, I'd do without sex easy."

"You can't do without sex for two minutes."

These fights were so stupid that we always ended by laughing as well as combining, and the fact is that we were crazy about each other and I knew that Masefield had grown to love the person that I was, the friend and mother and postmistress I was, as well as lover.

And I loved the man that was Masefield, although I truly didn't know him because there was a part of him that was unreachable, with which I could not connect. I don't think it was simply because he was so much smarter than me because, after all, I'd lived with Daddy, who was a genius, and we understood each other just fine and, although this might sound surprising, also Buster. I actually believe that Buster was head and shoulders the smartest man who ever walked the earth, even though he seemed so ordinary.

How I missed him. Oh, dear God, how I missed that man. And every time I think how he bicycled out of town and kept on going across the whole country, it breaks my heart. I think about Buster and feel terrible pain and guilt.

But what could I have done? I couldn't have told Masefield not to come. There was no way to tell him even if my heart had allowed it. Because I'd been *waiting* for him. Waiting for Masefield had become as much a part of my life as being with Buster and looking for Mom and wondering about Daddy. All these things were so integrated. Therefore, not letting Masefield arrive here would be like being given a chance to actually lay my hands on Mom and not doing it.

The waiting, of course, had seemed to give an added dimension to my life, a meaning, just as Mom's looking for Andy gives mad meaning to her life. But you can't let the obsession take over and be sufficient in itself. You have to fulfill the contract, go through with the deal, finish, close. If I'd been waiting years for Masefield to come, I couldn't, when it was finally happening, tell him not to come. That would be being a baby chicken.

I suddenly had the chilling realization that Bart, too, would have to kill Daddy if his life was to have meaning and not just be utter disintegration.

Because if you've saddled your life with some obsession of

waiting or looking or threatening, you've got to go through with the thing if it's to have any reality and not have been wasted time, wasted mind, even though it could end by being terribly destructive to others—not to mention to your own self.

This is what I thought as I sailed toward my Masefields. I knew that when I tried to tell Masefield about it, it would get garbled and sound stupid. Still, he would get what I was saying, because he was so good at making sense out of things, and he would know that that was another reason he loved me, because I thought about things and tried to tell him what they were.

But getting back to what started me off: I had to go through with Masefield coming, even if it meant Buster's suffering, or I would have diminished myself in my own eyes and, I believe, also in Buster's.

The day when M and I and Laurie were draggling back into town from having chased Buster, and I looked up and saw Masefield walking into town from the other side, I knew yes, this was right. It had to be this way. And I was scared too. Because everything would change now. Everything. And that's why I thought about suicide that night because I was just too scared to live no matter what happened and, in a way, too happy to live. And in another way it seemed that now Masefield had come, I could die, because the deal had at last closed.

But life goes on. There are new deals, new contracts, new things to saddle your mind and heart.

After our sail today, when Masefield and I could be alone again, I would tell him these thoughts I'd had while sailing toward him because I knew now that Bart would really kill Daddy if he came because obsessions become a point of pride to those driven by them. Even if you don't want to do a thing anymore, even if the obsession has just become a personal pet and comfort, you have to carry it to its conclusion because you've been talking of nothing else and you believe, wrongly, probably, that you'd let yourself and everyone else down, if you didn't close the deal.

"Hi, you guys," I said, throwing them the painter.

"Hey, Mom, do you know what he did?"

I felt so annoyed by M referring to his father as "he" that I just frowned instead of responding, but I wasn't going to find out anyhow because Masefield said, "Don't tell, M. It'll be our secret, okay?"

"Okay."

# 25. FINDING MUIR

The snow was falling in thick ploppy moist flakes. Each snowflake was the size of a pancake. The ocean, gray and gloomy, grumbled out beyond the harbor, which was mostly full of fishing boats. I felt tired, wet, cold, and lonely—which pretty much describes how I'd been feeling for the last three months, especially lonely.

I headed for a phone booth, my ongoing solace, propped my bike against it, dialed O, and gave the operator the number, feeling better by the second, even grinning as I heard the rings.

"Hi, Chris," I said happily. "It's me, Buster. Is M there?"

"No, he's gone sailing with Sunny and Masefield."

Massive disappointment. I couldn't speak.

"Where are you, Buster?"

Where was I? Good question. At the other end of the earth, it felt like. In no-man's-land. Everybody I cared about was so far away, endlessly far away. And there was just this greasy gray ocean in front of me and nowhere to go but into it. I'd leave the bike on shore. It was a pretty special bike.

Then I suddenly realized I could just turn my bike around right now as soon as I hung up and head west. Then every day I'd be getting closer to home, to Sunny and M, and I didn't care anymore about Masefield, he could be there or not, it didn't matter. It made my heart beat just to think about turning around and getting closer to them with every pedaling of the wheel. I even looked out at my bike to see if it was pointed the right way and therefore already getting closer. It was.

Finally I answered Chris. "I'm in Gloucester, Massachusetts, looking at the Atlantic Ocean. I've been hanging around this statue of a fisherman that says 'They that go down to the sea in ships.' I sort of don't know where to go now. I think I'll come home. I've got this great idea!"

It had just come to me. Like all my ideas, it just jumped into my mind for no particular reason.

"What is it?"

"Well, bicycling across the country, I kept stopping at different places, bike shops and machine shops, to make alterations, little improvements, on the bike, see. I even thought of a new kind of tire and got that made, and now everyone—other bicyclists, I mean—keeps stopping me to ask about my bike and where can they get one just like it, so now all I want to do is come home and start making the things. Ones like this one and a super innovative revolutionary bike I've been thinking about that will stand the world on its ear.

"I think bicycle racing is going to start being big in this country the way it is in Europe, the big tours and all."

Telling about it, I forgot about the cold and lonely part of the trip, all the misery, and just remembered the wonderful sights, the friendly people, the good exercise. "I've had the greatest time going across the country and I bet other people are going to start doing it too."

"It sounds like a really good idea, Buster."

"I'll rent a shop. I can't wait to tell M. He can help me. I don't know *how* exactly, but he can just come to the shop and stuff, just be there whenever he wants to. He's about ready for a two-wheeler anyhow; I don't know why we never got him one. Why didn't we?"

"He was always just happy to ride on the back of yours. He's only four, remember."

"Almost five."

"Listen, Buster," Chris said tentatively, "would you do something for me?"

"Sure."

"I think Muir Scott's in Gloucester now. I'd be so appreciative if you'd check up on him, see how he is. He has a cottage there that he built with his father when he was about your age, and I have a feeling that that's where he went when I left him. It's in Lanesville. Rowley Shore Road, which is a dirt road on the Ipswich Bay side."

I didn't want to, but what could I say? Chris was being so good about taking care of M. "Okay. Sure. Any message if I find him?"

"Tell him I . . . we (me, Laurie, M, and Sunny) all love him and to please come home."

I thought about that message and decided not to comment. Instead I asked, "What's happening with Sunny and Masefield?"

"I don't know, Buster. They never talk about the future, just live day to day."

"Any sightings of Mom?"

"Not for quite a while."

"How are you, Chris?"

"Oh, I'm fine. But I'm worried about Bart. You know how I go over there every week and clean his house and stock in food for him?"

"Yeah."

"Well, nothing's been touched for several weeks. I think he just wanders around the countryside and sleeps outside now. I think he's living like an animal."

"So am I. It's not so bad. It's a good way to live, under the sun and the stars. Maybe he's going back to being an Indian. It has to be the way Sunny's mom lives. She hasn't been indoors for five years now, as far as we know. And Masefield lived like an animal for four years in prison."

"I hope Muir's okay," she said sadly, and I remembered that she hadn't seen him for almost four years and here I was moaning to myself because of three months without Sunny and M.

"I'll let you know. I'll call you back tonight. Give M a big hug and kiss for me, okay? And tell him I'm coming home. I'm on my way!"

"You bet."

"Thanks, Chris, you're so wonderful."

"So are you. Bye Buster."

"Bye, Chris."

"Lanesville?" answered an old codger near the phone booth. "Just take route twenty-eight either direction and you'll come to it since the road goes in a circle. It's a right pretty ride either way."

Inside of an hour I was on Rowley Shore Road, a rocky pot-holed road that skirted the coast. There were chunks of ice and snow on it, too. The outermost cottage was Muir Scott's, and, asking directions, I'd already learned he was there.

I was in kind of a bad mood. I felt disappointed to be still heading east now that I'd gotten both ideas, the one of going home, the other of building bikes when I got there. Also, I didn't have any good feelings about Muir Scott.

First he'd abandoned Sunny's mom and then Sunny herself and finally, in a way, he'd abandoned Chris. It just seemed like the guy didn't know how to love anybody even though they loved him with all their hearts.

Then of course there was the fact that he'd never liked me hanging around Sunny to begin with. He had bigger plans for her, which turned out to be Masefield.

And then, I hated to think this, but what if there was something in what Bart kept saying, that Muir had killed Sunny's mom? I mean, why *had* the guy left Inverness since, if Chris was to be believed, Laurie wasn't his child and he never had anything going with her at any time?

The way I felt was: if he did kill her, that was pretty bad, but it could have been an accident. What was really bad, unforgivable, was if he had killed her and then set Sunny to looking for her as if her mom were still alive because for sure that had twisted up Sunny's whole life.

Still, I'd find him for Chris's sake and I'd give him the message from her and Sunny and maybe even Laurie, but not M, because how could M love him and miss him and want him to come home if he didn't even know him? I wasn't going to put words in M's mouth that hadn't really come from him to his grandfather, who'd ignored him all his life.

I wonder if the reason I'm so loving, so overloving, is that I have no family at all so everyone is super important to me. People with families take everyone for granted, take them or leave them, mostly leave them.

Even in this horrible weather, Muir Scott had apparently been out fishing in his dory. Now he was pulling the dory up onto the rocks about a hundred yards down from where I stood by his cottage. He wore a yellow slicker and yellow hat and he appeared to have a white beard. If it was even him.

He walked up the steep path with his bucket of fish in one hand and his gear in the other. There was a spring in his step and he looked strong. By now I figured it wasn't him because Muir Scott always moved so slowly.

But it was him. "Who the hell are you?" he asked, but it was friendly.

"Buster."

"Buster. Good grief! Come on in." He hung his slicker outside the door while I put my bike up on the porch. Watching me, he commented wryly, "Funny day to choose to bicycle around in."

"It was sunny and dry when I set out, three months ago," I commented back.

"Don't tell me you pedaled here from Inverness?"

"Yeah, I did."

"That's remarkable. Why?"

Since I didn't exactly know why, I just told him it had nothing to do with him and that I'd only fetched up here by chance and searched him out to please Chris. I gave him the message that she loved him and missed him and wanted him to come home but left Sunny and Laurie out of the message as well as M.

He didn't seem to be listening because he didn't respond to any of this but instead said, as he put a kettle of water on for tea, "As I was walking up the path from the rocks, I saw you standing there by the cottage and I felt catapulted into a time warp. I visited myself thirty-five years ago when I built this cottage with Pa. It was an out-of-body experience that was an out-of-time one, too. You were me and I was Pa. It about gave me a stroke and then I thought maybe I *was* having a stroke and that's why I was scrambling the fourth dimension." He pondered. "I actually do look quite a lot like Pa now, come to think of it, now that I'm strong again and grew this beard." He stroked it.

"Don't you want to hear about Chris and Sunny?" I asked. "Don't you want to hear about your grandchild?"

"No." He sighed. "Not particularly." He threw some tea leaves in a pot and filled it up. He took two big bowllike cups down from a shelf.

"Why not?"

He looked at me sort of startled. I guess I sounded angry. Well, I was angry. Damned angry. "I'll tell you why not," I said. "Because you're a fool. You're a stupid old fool.

"You asked me why I pedaled all the way across the country and I didn't know what to say. But now I know why I did it. It was so I could tell you you're the biggest fool who ever lived."

The man was looking at me, stunned.

"Here you have the most wonderful daughter in the whole world, a woman made of golden light. Golden sweetness and light. And you've got a little grandson who's a prince. He's so cute. He's so darn cute and adorable." I was starting to cry. "And he can run really fast for his age. And he wants to go everywhere with you and do everything that you do, even though he's not anywhere near big enough, even though his hands are so little. Still, I gave him a miniature tool set and... But never mind that. You've also got Chris, who's a fine woman and cares for you a lot, God knows why, and her little Laurie. You've got all those people who love you and want you home with them (Darn! I was giving Chris's whole message after all), and you don't give a hoot in hell for any of them. You don't even *particularly* want to hear about them. And who have I got? Nobody. No family at all. Nobody in the world who wants me home. Except little M. M does. But he's just a little kid and he'll forget about me soon. He's probably out sailing around right now with Sunny and Masefield and not thinking a thing about me."

"M?"

"Your grandson!" I shouted. "See! You don't even know his name!"

He pushed me gently into the chair. "Sit down and drink your tea."

I sat down and was suddenly overcome with exhaustion. I wanted to sleep for a million years. I laid back my head.

Muir Scott opened the doors of the Franklin stove. There was a fire inside. He added some small logs and it flared up. Then he sat down across from me. "You're right," he said. "I'm a stupid old fool." He looked at me with an all-enveloping gaze. "Thank you."

When I woke up, it was dark. The wind was howling around the little cottage. For a minute I thought I was back in the water house. Then I saw Muir, reading by the light of a dim lamp. "What time is it?" I asked. "I never called Chris. I promised her I'd call if I found you."

"It's ten o'clock, but just seven o'clock there. Feel free to use my phone since, as of a few hours ago, I stopped hiding out."

"I'm sorry I said all those things to you. I was so tired when I arrived and I was feeling mad at you in my heart. The fact is, I don't like you very much and I shouldn't be accepting your hospitality."

"That's all right. I don't like you, either. Never have." He smiled at me again and in spite of myself, I smiled back. We both laughed. It was a pretty funny situation. He pointed to the phone so I got up and used it. Chris answered and as soon as I said, "It's Buster," she started talking nonstop.

"Thank God you've called. You've got to come right home. There's been an accident. Sunny's boat."

"No!" I gasped. "No!"

"They were running in heavy air and as the boat jibed it went into what they call a death roll."

"No! Oh, God!"

"It's when you jibe the boat and the boom comes across and the boat starts a series of oscillations, rolling back and forth so that you can't stop it and then it just turns turtle, just turns over completely. It can happen to the best of sailors."

"Sunny's okay, isn't she? She's not hurt? And oh, God, what about little M?"

"Sunny was knocked unconscious and she has a concussion. She's in the hospital now. She's still unconscious, but the doctor thinks she'll be coming out of it pretty soon."

"I'll grab a plane tonight. I'll get back as soon as I can. Oh, Sunny, Sunny!"

"Wait. There's more. Masefield saved Sunny first of all because he knew she'd been knocked out. He had to dive for her and it all took a few minutes but then he couldn't see M anywhere. M had on his life preserver and Masefield figured he'd be bobbing around nearby but he wasn't. Then Masefield got scared that M maybe was caught under the boat but he didn't dare let go of Sunny. Finally he got her over the boat bottom and dove under for M, but he wasn't there. He wasn't anywhere. There were big waves. It was hard to see. Naturally he called and called. . . ."

"But what are you saying, Chris? They've found him now, haven't they? Is he there with you now?"

"No, he isn't. We haven't found him, Buster."

## 26. FINDING M

This blighted place. I felt that I was imprisoned in a Greek drama, the plot of which inexorably unwound with none of the characters having any will or say, the chorus in the background maniacally prognosticating more grief and tragedy and madness.

I remembered back some six years or so ago when my father showed me a photo. "That's Muir Scott," he said, "my old classmate from Harvard. Have you read his stuff?"

"Yes, but who is that with him?"

"That's his daughter, Sunny."

"I want to meet her," I said.

Then I met her in Paris, a pretty teenager, a simple sailor girl from a one-horse town in California, and I fell in love just while standing there at her pension door introducing myself, never dreaming that coming with the territory of her simple youth and beauty, which was like sunlight on the sea, were subterranean wells of darkness, dread, and horror. Within two weeks, her mother had gone mad, maybe had been murdered by her father, who had fled with her best friend pregnant with someone's child, maybe his, and we ourselves had created a child within that time. During the next year our child was born and I was imprisoned because of having spared a girl who reminded me of her. Then four years of grace for Sunny until I could come to her in Inverness and set the plot in motion again, the plot that had grown so incredible as to be grotesque, her child lost in the bay just as her own little brother had been. Now what? Now would Sunny go mad in the footsteps of her mother, the *wake* of her mother? Would she even come to consciousness again? Should she?

She had awakened once. During her first hour at the hospital, while the doctor was running tests on her, she came to and demanded to know about M and me. Upon learning M was lost, she'd grown so hysterical that the doctor had to give her a needle—which perhaps wasn't too wise on top of her concussion.

Now I stared down at her lifeless face. The doctor said it was a light coma; she would come to when she was ready. But maybe she'd never be ready. Maybe, now that she knew M was lost, she didn't want to come to.

Why come to, just so as to go mad?

I kissed her cold lips. "Listen, Sunny, if you've lost little M, we'll leave this place. Together. We'll put miles between us and Inverness. I'll drop my career. We'll go where there are waters to sail and the sun always shines. Okay, we'll go where there's lots of fog, too. Anywhere, just so that you can stay sane and loving. We'll have more kids. It's true I'll hate it. It's true that's not at all what I want my life to be. But I don't care anymore. It will be worth it to foil the inexorable plot, to exercise our wills against the great dramatist in the sky who's so shittily composing our ill-starred lives. It will be worth it to keep you well and happy."

But that's exactly what Muir Scott said one mustn't do. He said you can't take care of a person, can't spend your life looking after someone. You end by subsuming your personality into the state of affairs. When you think you're being calm and kind and forbearing, not to mention philosophical, you're really depressed as hell from all the held-in anger.

I couldn't stand to begin to hate Sunny, to resent her, maybe to . . . (a chill swept over me) to murder her. Better to brutally leave her to her fate than to initiate the one that the evil playwright may have in mind all along in this hideous repetition of blighted history.

I felt a hand on my shoulder. It was Chris. "Masefield," she said, "it's morning. Let me sit with Sunny and you go on back to Inverness for some breakfast and some rest. Okay? Go on, Masefield. Really."

Not that Chris had had any rest. There were black circles under her eyes. "Any word?" I asked hopelessly. She shook her head.

"Thing is," she said, "the water's so cold in February. He just wouldn't have lasted very long in that cold water."

"Still, they'd find him. He'd be floating."

"Right."

"And they haven't found him."

"Right."

Two hopeless-sounding people.

"How's little Laurie doing?"

"Crying her eyes out. She says she knew yesterday morning that it was going to happen because it felt just like the day M went running after Buster—when she thought she was going to lose M forever."

"God," I said despairingly. "How can little four-year-olds be so tragic? And Buster?"

"He's here—on his way from the airport. And Muir's coming in a week or so."

"Really?"

"Yes." She shook her head. "It could have been an occasion for rejoicing, but now it can't be. Now nothing can be, maybe ever."

From the hospital I took Highway 101 to the Lucas Valley turnoff and followed the road to Inverness. Once there I stopped at the coffee shop for some breakfast but couldn't eat. People came up and commiserated with me. Everyone knew. Everyone asked after Sunny and didn't dare mention M. Instead they would look dolefully out at the bay.

If they said anything, it was, "It's good they haven't found him," meaning maybe he wasn't dead. Meaning as long as they didn't have a body he could still be alive.

But they hadn't found Andy, either. Tell me that was "good."

Through my connections with the government, I'd been able

to employ the U.S. Army stationed at the Presidio in San Francisco to help in the search. There wasn't a square inch of the bay or the land around it that wouldn't be searched. By the end of the day we'd have a body, alive or dead, to present to Sunny when she came to.

I went out to the water house. I would throw myself down on the bed for an hour and then go on back to the hospital.

The door was open as usual, and there on the bed was little Laurie, sitting rather primly on the edge and looking quite important. "Hi, Laurie. Are you okay? Do you think this is a good place for you to be?"

"I'm taking care of M."

Oh, man, don't tell me Laurie's gone over the edge now. Is no one to be spared?

"He's very cold and sleepy," she said. She pronounced it "sweepy."

I noticed a tiny mound of blankets in the center of the bed and my heart leaped. Don't get excited, I cautioned myself. Laurie might have made that little mound with a pillow or two.

But the pillows were on the bed in their usual place.

"Laurie, are you telling me..."

She held up her hand imperiously. "Don't wake him! I *promised* I'd let him sleep."

I was so afraid she was pretending. I was pretty sure she was pretending, playing dolls, playing M was alive and in her care. In an exaggerated tiptoe, I went over and lifted a corner of the blanket and there was M, sure enough, snoozing away, looking slightly the worse for wear, but definitely a live little four-year-old boy going on five. I put my finger on his neck for a pulse and it was fine and steady.

It gave me a lump in my throat. Right then I knew I loved the kid.

I reached for the phone to call the hospital right away, but then I thought how much better to go and tell Sunny myself, wake her with the good news. It would only take me half an hour to get there if I drove like crazy, and it would be much the better way. She wouldn't believe just anyone telling her.

Then I began to allow myself to feel this incredible happiness.

M was alive. He was okay. And Sunny was going to be okay, too. Life could go on. There wasn't going to be a tragedy for any of us.

"Listen, Laurie, I want to go and tell Sunny and Chris. Can you keep watching over M?"

"Of course."

"You won't let him out of your sight?"

"Nope."

"Okay. Hold the fort, then." I started out the door, then thought to ask, "Where did you find him?"

"He was walking down the road."

As I drew near Sunny's hospital room I heard a voice that sounded too low to be Chris's. It was Buster. He'd gotten onto Sunny's bed and was lying down beside her holding her in his arms. I'd forgotten how huge he was. She looked so slight, so ethereal in his arms, like a long-stemmed flower fallen on the thick knobby branch of a tree. He was holding her in his arms and rocking her gently. She was still unconscious, but he was talking to her a mile a minute. He looked scared to death. He looked like he didn't know where he was or what was happening. His eyes were turned up in his head. He was talking to her on and on, senselessly. He was talking in their secret language.

# 27. FINDING MOM

Where was I? What was happening?

I came to, thinking it was an earthquake. My bed was dancing across the room.

Even stranger was the actual cause. Buster was on the bed beside me and Masefield was bending over him shaking him, saying intensely, "Quit it! Shut up!"

"What? What?" Buster was saying.

I joined in the chorus. "What?"

"Sunny!" said Masefield.

"What's happening? Why are you shaking Buster?"

"What?" said Buster.

"He was having a fit," Masefield answered me.

"Sunny?" said Buster.

"Fit?" I asked Masefield.

"Sunny, you're awake!" Buster said, looking surprised to find himself lying beside me on the bed, taking up the whole thing, me sort of clinging to the edge of it at this point.

"We found M. He's home," Masefield said quickly.

It took a second to penetrate and then I burst into tears.

"Oh, thank you, Masefield, thank you!" Buster said, also bursting into tears. He got to a sitting position and clasped

Masefield's hands. I think he even kissed them, but it was hard to tell through my tears. One thing I *could* tell was that Buster hadn't changed a bit when it came to being emotional.

"I didn't find him," Masefield said, looking stern as if it were his duty to offset all the emotion running rampant in the room. "Laurie did. Or, I don't know, I think he just walked home from somewhere. Anyhow"—he gave up the austerity and smiled happily—"he's in the water house fast asleep and Laurie's watching over him. I haven't heard his story because I didn't want to wake him. I just wanted to get the hell back here and tell you."

I sat up. It about killed my head to do so, but I didn't want to show the pain. I sat there, reeling, but managed to say, "Let's go!"

"You're not going anywhere," Masefield said with what seemed like unnecessary ferocity. "You've got a concussion. You've been in a goddamn coma, for Christ's sake."

Buster looked surprised that Masefield would talk to me so harshly. He should be around for one of our fights.

"I'm going," I said doggedly. "I'm not going to be a baby chicken about this."

Masefield looked puzzled, so Buster explained gently, looking at me with pride, "Champs can't be baby chickens. It's not allowed."

Masefield looked at me and said in a voice that completely cowed me, a new voice I'd never heard in all our exchanges, "You're staying."

"I can lie down just as well at home as I can here," I beseeched him. "I want to see M so bad. Please?"

"I'll carry you to the car," Buster said. "I'll carry her," he told Masefield as if that would take care of all his objections, and before Masefield could remonstrate, Buster swooped me into his arms.

Naturally we got hassled on our way out of the hospital, me with a bandaged head in a hospital gown and all. But Buster just bulled his way through, carrying me, and Masefield trailed after explaining. He was a fast talker when he wanted to be and also could be very officious and intimidating. He could show people cards that would stop them dead in their tracks. For all I knew, he was the head of the FBI.

For some reason, maybe because of seeing him with his take-charge personality, I thought, Poor Masefield hasn't seen an opera in so long. He might as well still be in prison. He's all well now. He can go now if he wants to because he's well. That new voice was probably his old voice he just got back. His working voice.

As for me, I thought, I'm out for the count, a champion biting the dust, but that's okay because M's found and Buster's come home to us. Even if Masefield goes, everything's going to be okay.

Buster looked happy too. He was smiling his head off. What a guy! There was no one like Buster.

They wanted to lay me down in the backseat, but I didn't want to be alone in the back or leave one of them alone in the front so I wedged in between them. I figured we'd all been through a lot in the last twenty-four hours and should stick close together. They'd been through the worst of it because they'd had the worry while I'd been happily out cold. However, I could remember the time I woke up, when they told me M was lost. I remembered my thoughts then and spoke them now.

"Masefield, remember when I woke up in the hospital and started screaming away?"

"Yes. My ears will never forget it. They're still reverberating."

"It was because of M being lost, of course, but it was something else too."

"Yes?"

"It was Buster. All I could think, Buster"—I turned now to him—"was how it would kill you if M was lost and how I wouldn't be able bear your grief, your monumental grief, and how I would always feel to blame. I know your love for M is greater even than mine. Then, I had this incredible realization about Mom. That it was the same thing with her. It wasn't that she loved Andy so much that she went mad. She went mad because of Daddy's grief and feeling to blame. All these years she hasn't just been looking for Andy. Mom's been looking for Andy for Daddy. So she could give him back to him."

After I got all this off my chest I fell asleep on someone's shoulder and the next thing I knew, Buster was carrying me down the pier to the house.

M was still sleeping. Laurie was drawing pictures. One by one we tiptoed to the bed and peered down at his sleeping face, his little scrunched-up form. I lay down beside him and the others found places and talked in hushed voices.

Buster called Chris at work to tell her the news and Masefield opened some cans of soup for lunch.

Here I was with all my dear family (except Chris, who was only just down the road), and I felt so happy, so lucky. We were all together. All safe and sound.

Except for Daddy and Mom, of course, but I realized they didn't matter so much now. My family was here in Buster, Masefield, Chris, Laurie, and M. Life goes on. In a way, I hadn't been letting it go on. Now I would. Now I knew what mattered. What mattered was . . . was . . . this. This that I was feeling now. And if ever I got really down or scared or wanting to die, I would say to myself, No, don't feel like that, you idiot, remember this.

Even Masefield going away wasn't going to kill me. He'd come back. He loved me. The only real way you lost someone was death. Death and, I guess, madness.

Buster wasn't being quite as quiet as he should. I knew he was dying for M to wake up. He'd drop something or bump something and go, "Oops! Sorry!" in a loud whisper, and so, pretty soon he succeeded in waking him and of course M went into a complete delirium of joy to see Buster.

Buster cried again. He was the most emotional man who ever lived.

We all had our lunch and then, with M on Buster's lap, me lying down on the bed, and the others sitting on the bed with me, including Chris, who had got off work, M told his story.

*Which was that Mom had saved him.*

That's what he told us.

He said he'd floated around a while getting pretty cold, and then a lady in a boat had come, a white-haired lady in a boat who looked just like me only with lots of wrinkles, had sailed up to him, pulled him aboard, and taken him to the dock of my family house and then he'd gone into the house to take off his wet clothes so as to get dry and stop shivering (he was a little fuzzy here as to whether she'd come in the house with him or left him at the dock) and by then it was dark and he wasn't real sure how to get home even though he'd come there lots of times with Buster, and the phone didn't work, so he just went to sleep until morning, when he got up early, put on his damp clothes, and found his way the two miles to town.

We all stayed quiet for a while after hearing all this, thinking our own thoughts and being, for the most part, pretty astounded. Then we began looking at each other to see what the other person would say.

The thing was that M had spent the whole of his short life hearing about this woman on the bay and looking for her with me, and he could have imagined the whole thing pretty easily and somehow just fetched up at the dock himself.

It was weird how I, who had totally believed all this while, all these years, that Mom was really out there, couldn't believe the story because it simply seemed too incredible. But it was a wonderful story, too.

It was Chris who spoke first. She ran her hand through the field of hair on her head and said pensively, "Maybe your mom will come home now."

"Why, Chris?" I asked.

"Well, because maybe she thinks she found Andy."

"That's right. She could think that, couldn't she? Because, in her madness, it's always the day he was lost. And M's Andy's age. It would explain why she returned him to Andy's house, not this one."

"Or maybe she'll die now," Masefield said. And when we all looked at him kind of shocked, he explained. "Your father said (it was when we met in The Bar Central) that looking for Andy was the only thing that kept her going, gave meaning to her life, even if it was mad meaning."

We all got quiet again, turning this over in our minds. I wanted to tell everyone my great realization that Mom was really looking for Andy for Daddy, but it might confuse things even more. I would tell them all later. I'd already told Masefield and Buster, so that was good.

"I actually don't believe M's story," Masefield said. "What I think is that M imagined her. But who cares? He's home. That's the main thing."

"How come you believed about the albatross, then?" M asked, looking at his father with accusing eyes, the same purple eyes with long black lashes.

We were all mystified by the reference, so Masefield briefly told us the count's albatross story he'd told M yesterday, just before the sail. Only yesterday!

"I don't believe *that* story one bit," said Buster to Masefield but looking at me. He hadn't once stopped looking at me unless it was to look at M. "It's the unlikeliest thing I ever heard. Are you kidding? Grab hold of an albatross?"

Masefield smiled. I was so glad of his way with Buster. He was being really nice. I suddenly remembered him shaking Buster and wondered what that had all been about. "It is a pretty wild story," he agreed. "But if you knew the count, and heard him tell it, you'd believe it. He's bigger than life."

Then little Laurie said, "You know what I think?" and waited. When we all respectfully asked her "What?" she said, "I think it was Mom's ghost. I bet she's dead and her ghost haunts the bay. But now it won't have to anymore," she added, loyally incorporating her mother's idea, "because she's found Andy."

That was a rather nice idea, somehow satisfying, if you just looked at it as an idea. If you looked at it as truth, it gave you goose bumps. Because if she had died, when did she? How did she? To think of her poor ghost restlessly flitting over the bay, in a ghost boat to boot . . . well . . .

"It was Mom's mom," M said definitively, but not necessarily furthering our understanding.

"Right," said Buster, summing it all up. "It certainly sounds like she's alive and out there on the bay just like we always thought. And the chances are good that she thinks she found Andy and she'll be coming home. Maybe she's there now." For the *first time* he took his eyes off me and M and looked out at the bay. "Boy," he said, "look how green the hills are. In New England everything is stone-colored."

I thought again about Masefield shaking Buster and remembered Masefield saying that Buster was having a fit and I was just going to ask him about what exactly this fit had constituted when Chris told me a rather major piece of news, which was that Daddy was coming home.

I guess it was just too much to handle on top of everything else because I fell asleep again and pretty much stayed asleep, for the next five days.

Before I dropped off, however, I had this memory, this glimmering, shimmering wisp of a memory about a thought I'd had, that I'd meant to impart to Masefield after the sail about why it was essential that Daddy not come home.

I couldn't get a handle on what it was, though. Maybe it would come to me when I woke up.

# 28. SLEEPING

I had the most wonderful sleep. It was a dreamy time. Let's see, five days would be one hundred and twenty hours of sleep interspersed with enough moments of awakenings to subtract only a few hours all told.

That was what made it so great, the fact that I woke up only to go back to sleep again. I would wake up just long enough to eat or go to the bathroom or make love to Masefield or tell whoever was there that I was all right.

It was part of the dreamy wonderfulness to see who would be there, what time of day it was, what the weather was like, to sort of notice all this, as if to reestablish my tiny toehold on reality before drifting off to sleep again.

Sometimes I would awake to the rising sun showering my bed with warmth and light and see Masefield in a shadowy corner, bent over his chessboard or a book, steam rising from his coffee mug, smoke issuing from his cigarette or mouth.

Sometimes my eyes would open to the dim light of evening with a flight of brown pelicans streaming by the window as if their putting a hole through the air with their beaks and bodies had awakened me. Or it might be the lone shape of a cormorant on the end of the pier disturbing my slumber by the force of its brooding stillness. Or the silly orioles. The moon. The dark rain clouds.

Maybe it would be the silver water in the morning mist, the green hills also silvered, awakening me by their change of color or else, in the noon sun, by the ferocity of their greenness seeping through my eyelids, merging into my mind.

More often than not I would awake to the bulk of Buster, lying beside me, keeping watch over me during some odd hour of the day. I would behold his dear face, smile, and sleep some more.

It would not be unusual to spot Masefield somewhere in the room at the same time. Or, reversed positions, Masefield beside me, Buster in the kitchen or at the table. The men seemed wholly comfortable with each other. In my dreamy state it seemed to me that they loved each other.

M might be sitting on the bed beside me, drawing. I might wake to his crayoned creation held in my face, rousing me with its color in the same way as the hills.

These were the things that awakened me, everything but sound. They told me later that there was no rousing me if anyone had something they badly needed to say. Two or three or four of them could be talking to beat the band two feet away and I'd sleep through every word.

Sometimes, rarest of all, but sometimes, I'd awake because I had something I wanted to say. It was always the same two things, the two realizations: that Mom had really been looking for Andy for Daddy. And that if Daddy came home, Bart was going to shoot him.

Mostly, deep in the heart of the night, the silent swell of Masefield's penis would pierce my slumber, or the moon groping its way through the clouds would, or the loyal lovelight in Buster's eyes would, always always always would.

# 29. THE GARDEN

When I was young, I saw a movie called *The Secret Garden*. It was in black and white until a certain door was opened to the secret garden, at which point the movie turned Technicolor.

That's how it was when I went to Sunny's old home to investigate (finally getting off my ass to investigate, after five years,) leaving Sunny deep in her ongoing sleep, her cop-out sleep, I called it, since, if she woke up, she would have to come to grips with Buster being back and her father coming home—because it was a foggy black-and-white day until I stepped through the gate to the garden and then it was a knock-your-eyes-out Technicolor display of spring flowers: daffodils, tulips, lilies, lilac, Scotch broom, plum blossoms, cherry blossoms, Japanese quince. Those were just the ones I knew.

Buster and M were there, working away. They hadn't noticed me enter, so I was able to observe them. Everything Buster had —wheelbarrow, hoe, spade, trowel, rake—M had in miniature, probably hand-forged by Buster. And M wasn't playing; he was working—in miniature, but definitely working. They were both intense and serious. I could tell by the way they gardened together, and by the garden itself, that this wasn't work of just the last week since Buster got home, but of years.

When I had announced myself and commented on what I saw, Buster told me he'd been taking care of the garden for Mom ever since Sunny had got home from Paris and M had been helping him ever since he could walk. "But now I'm behind on my spring weeding. With Mom maybe coming home now and Muir coming for sure, M and I have got to get hopping." He grinned. "Gardening's great." He gestured at the panorama of color. "It's so rewarding."

Buster, on his hands and knees, M standing close beside him covered with dirt, was a picture of happiness. Sure he loved gardening. And bicycling and plumbing and carpentering and oystering and Sunny and M. What didn't he love? *Whom* didn't he love? He probably even loved me.

"Chris is inside, cleaning," Buster said. "Hey, M, why don't you go get yourself some lemonade? Take a break."

M scampered off. "You can forget Sunny's mom coming home," I said. "I'm almost positive she's dead."

Buster squatted back on his huge haunches, wiping his hands on his knees, looking up at me. He had moisture on his face that was part sweat, part fog. "M just saw her," he reminded me.

"M's crazy," I answered, lighting a cigarette. "You're all crazy. This whole town is crazy."

"What about the Freedom riders?" he surprised me by asking. "Are they crazy? No. They believe in something. So do we. We believe Mom's alive and living in a boat on the bay. There have been a whole bunch of sightings. Everyone's seen her at one time or another. Sunny talked to her. M was lifted out of the bay by her."

When he talked like that, being so positive and hopeful, it made me want to be brutal. Or maybe I wanted to be brutal because I never believed in anything in my whole life. As far as I was concerned, as far as I *knew*, there was nothing at all in the world to believe in, although there was a hell of a lot to be examined. So I said, "I think Muir killed her."

Buster hung his head, looking saddened.

"I think you think so, too, Buster. I think you think a lot of things that you don't ever say. Anyhow, I'm going to find out."

"How? Are you going to ask him?"

"I don't think he knows. I think he did it, maybe accidentally, and repressed it."

"Then it would kill him to learn for sure that she was dead. And how would Sunny handle learning such a thing as that her father killed her mother?"

"Maybe they don't need to know, Buster. For sure they don't want to know. But I do."

"Why?"

"I like to know things . . . just to know. Not because I'm necessarily going to do anything with the knowledge."

"Because it gives you power over people?" Buster suggested, not unkindly.

"It does give me power over people, but that's not why I do it. I want to know things because . . ." I thought for a minute, then smiled. "It makes me happy. The way gardening makes you happy. It's rewarding. Anyhow, I am connected to you all, don't forget. This is my life too. These are my son's grandparents we're talking about."

I put out my cigarette, tearing up the butt so as not to defile the garden. Then I said tentatively, "Buster, wouldn't you like to know about your youth, the part you've forgotten?"

I looked at him closely. It could well be that he knew subconsciously and very close to consciously that he was Andy but couldn't bear to acknowledge it because it would mean he could no longer love Sunny in the way that he did. It would mean a major readjustment in his life to become a brother to Sunny and, for that matter, a son to Muir.

"Why bother? I'd still be Buster," he said easily. "It wouldn't change who I am now. Lots of people can't remember a whole lot about their youth. I know because I've asked people."

"What if something had happened to M on the bay that was so awful it made him forget everything, made him forget you?"

"He'd still be M. He'd still have all the good in him of my and Sunny's love." Buster laughed. "I'd sure hate him to forget me, though. On the bicycle trip I kept being afraid he'd forget me. It would be awful to be forgotten. But"—he smiled—"I'm here to say that it's really not so bad to be the forgetter."

He got up, trundled the wheelbarrow over to the compost heap, and dumped the weeds.

He doesn't know, I decided. Or else (in a flash of illumination) he does know and has known for long enough, maybe for years, to learn to live with it by denying it. He denies it with all the full force of his Busterhood, because it damn well doesn't suit him to be Andy.

Being a person as good, as nice, as Buster, contrary to what some people think, didn't make him any kind of emotional wimp. This was a powerful personality here, an individual, a nonconformist. I'd discovered in my study of men that the good-hearted ones are always the strongest, the most courageous, the most intelligent, i.e., clear thinking, because they're unfettered by ambition, greed, fear, and all the other crummy needs humans are heir to that drag us down and make us act craven or base.

"How are you going to investigate?" he asked me, returning with a watering can and fertilizer, which he set down by the roses.

"I've asked a hot diver, a college buddy of mine, to come and look for Mom's boat. I'm meeting him and his assistant at the dock in fifteen minutes. He will be unobtrusive and no one will know what he's doing. If they ask, we'll say he's looking for old oyster trays."

Buster nodded. "That's possible."

"It will probably take a few days. They'll do the pole and string method, one holding a pole and the other searching the area around the pole in the circumference of the string. This will be very thorough, and from talking to Bart, I have a pretty good idea where the boat went down."

"You believe Bart?"

"Yes, I do. The man's gone mad. He's a man in the grip of an obsession all right, but that's not to say there's no truth in it. In fact, it's to say there probably is."

"He vowed to kill Muir if he ever came back, you know. At least that was his original intention five years ago, and I think the intention has grown stronger."

"I'm going to carry a gun and bodyguard Muir until we see what's what."

"You know how to shoot?"

"I know how to shoot."

"When's Muir getting here?"

"I'm picking him up at the airport Wednesday morning. I just hope we can wake up Sleeping Beauty by then."

Wednesday morning, I hauled Sunny out of bed, set her on her feet, and poured coffee down her throat. I walked her up and down and gave her more coffee along with some firm instructions.

"You are to stay awake. Your father's coming home this morning. I'm going to get him at the airport now."

"All right. Stop talking to me as if I were brain-damaged."

"How do you feel?"

"I feel scared because I'm going to have to tell him my two realizations."

"That Mom was looking for Andy for him?"

"Yes."

"That's pretty scary all right."

"Masefield, you're making fun."

"Okay, I don't see why Mom looking for Andy for Daddy is scary. Somehow it doesn't make my short hairs stand up or set my heart to racing. Sorry."

"Because Daddy didn't know how much she loved *him*, that her madness was for him, not for herself. Don't you understand?" She could see that I didn't and looked disappointed. "You usually always understand."

"Try me on the second scary realization."

"That Bart will kill Daddy."

"Oh, yeah, that one. You told me every time you woke up. What's new about that? Bart's been saying that for years and he's a loony tunes."

"But Masefield, you see, I realized he'll have to go through with it now that Daddy's come. He could just happily go on threatening until the cows came home as long as Daddy never showed up, but if he comes . . ."

"Bart's out roaming the countryside somewhere. He'll probably never run into him."

"I wonder why you're wearing your gun, then."

"I've got to go now. Are you going to stay awake?"

"I'm afraid so."

"I love you, Sunny."

"I love you, too."

I picked Muir up at the airport and drove him to Inverness. He looked very well, quite different with his beard and fit body. Maybe Bart wouldn't recognize him. Chris had said she would greet him later at his house, after he'd settled in, but I was going to bring him by the water house first, to see Sunny.

I stayed in the car while Muir walked the long pier to Sunny's house so they could have their reunion alone. I hoped she wasn't going to hit him with her scary realizations right off the bat. I hoped she was going to let him unpack first.

Fifteen minutes later he came back, looking pleased, so she either didn't tell him her scary realizations or she did and he wasn't very scared by them. Maybe he just sat by her bed and looked at her while she slept.

"Was she awake?" I asked.

"Sort of." He smiled.

We went on to his house. This whole return of his to Inverness had to be rather traumatic, but the Old Man from Harvard was handling it pretty well.

I carried in his bags and we went in the back way, which meant going through the garden. When he saw the garden he let out a cry.

I remembered him saying to me, that day we were together in The Bar Central, "Masefield, I want, just once, to feel so glad and surprised, that I knock over a chair, or suddenly change languages." His was a cry of gladness and surprise.

"It's happened, sir," I said.

He turned and I saw that his face was actually quivering with emotion. "What?" he asked. "What has happened, Masefield?"

I reminded him of what he had said, then added, "If you had entered this garden in a chair, you would have jumped up and knocked it over, changing languages while you were at it."

"Yes, yes, you're right." He started walking along the garden path, looking wonderingly at the flower beds like a man looking at the stained-glass windows of a cathedral. "You are entirely right, and the reason is that I have not walked in this garden since Andy died."

He took out a handkerchief to mop his face and eyes and I remembered that, too, from The Bar Central and how I'd entertained the idea of sporting a hanky myself. How young I was then. What an idiot.

"We worked in this garden together, Andy and I," Muir was saying. "We worked in it every single day of his life and this was how it looked. Yes, this is pretty much how it looked then, but it changed radically under the care of his mother when she took it over. Although I never came into it again, I would sometimes send it an involuntary glance as I passed. She simply didn't know enough to keep it up the way Andy and I had because we, you see, Andy and I, were botanists, while she . . . she was a sailor. Do you see what I'm saying, Masefield? This garden has returned to its former glory and not in a day. No, not in a day, and not by just anyone. Andy is alive."

That was all very well. That would certainly account for his emotion, his cry of gladness, and God knew, which is to say, I knew, it was true that Andy was alive. But the emotion he was experiencing was more complex than that, for then he got that same mad look on his face that they all (even little M) did when they mentioned her (at least to my eyes) as he said, "She must have found him," meaning, I suppose, that Sunny's mom finally, in all her senseless sailing, had come across Andy floating in his life jacket, which had burst the seams as he'd grown to manhood, and she'd hauled him in and set him straight to work in the garden. I didn't point out the gigantic flaws in his reasoning. He might as well think what he wanted to think. Everyone else around here did.

He looked around the garden again with wondering, astounded, thrilled eyes. "She wasn't crazy," he said, "she was right."

I thought to myself: She was crazy, she was right, and she was dead.

# 30. THE GARDEN, CONTINUED

"Laurie and I want to move in with you," Chris told me. "I could keep house for you, stop being a waitress, get my B.A., and then go on for a degree in psychology. Living with you will be an advanced degree in itself."

"It sounds like a good plan," I agreed. "We get along fine and it looks like I'm staying here in Inverness. At least everyone seems to assume I am and feel that I should. I guess I want to, too. But," I warned her, "I will go back to Lanesville for a while each summer and be by myself."

She smiled. "That's fair," she said.

"I think I am going to write a book," I said.

"It's about time. I'll help with that, too. I'm very excited at the idea of getting educated."

"I wish Sunny were," I said glumly.

"Sunny's done very well for herself. You should be proud of Sunny. Life hasn't been easy for her."

"You're right. It's not every woman who has two husbands and no wedding licenses."

We were sitting out in the garden as we talked. It was my second day home. Last night I learned from Sunny that it was Buster who looked after the garden. This left me dumbfounded.

I began to think my reaction upon first viewing it was hysteria of some sort, and now, being in it, I saw that it was just a garden, a lovely garden, but not supernaturally so. Probably all the stress of coming home had led me to behave in such a peculiar manner, which, luckily, only Masefield had observed.

Although I do not think of myself as an hysterical type. Perhaps it was a time warp I experienced, much like the one in Lanesville when I thought I was my father. And yet, and yet... that had to do with Buster, too!

A couple of robins were worming in the ground near our feet. I remembered about wishing on the first robin of spring. It seemed to me I had everything I could wish for. I was very touched that Chris wanted to live with me, be my helpmeet, amanuensis, and char. It occurred to me that I might tell her I was touched.

I looked at her where she sat in a splash of watery morning sun. "Chris, I'm very pleased that you want to be with me."

"I'm glad you'll have me. And it will be wonderful for Laurie to live with you. Also, I think you should consider being my lover at long last. I'm twenty-five years old now, I'm free, I'm not pregnant, and, more important, I love you."

This was even more touching. And I admired how she didn't mince words, wasn't coy. Nevertheless I felt it incumbent upon me to shake my head sadly and say, "It's not natural for a girl your age to be with an old man."

"It's plenty natural if she loves him."

"Sunny's mother is the only woman I've ever had sex with." I offered this fact up tentatively, not sure where it would lead me, where I wanted it to lead.

"Would you feel unfaithful to her?"

"No."

"Muir, do you feel scared to have sex with me?"

I thought about that and found it wasn't so. I yearned for some affection, some intimacy, and the object of this yearning seemed to take the form of Chris. "No," I answered.

The next thing I knew, Chris stood before me, leaned over, and pressed her lips against mine. Then she took me by the hand and led me back into the house, to Sunny's old bedroom, the single bed. For some reason, maybe because she was leading me, I felt like a child, a toddler.

She actually exclaimed with pleasure when she saw my body. All my hiking and rowing of the last years had got it looking pretty decent. I was glad for her sake.

Her body was dark and lithe, boyish, her breasts had scarcely any swell to them, but her nipples, as if to make up, were full and bright.

Feeling in no hurry, we lay together in the slender bed, hugging and kissing and talking. It was nice. I felt wonderfully well, neither young nor old. I didn't think of anything or anyone, only closed my eyes and experienced the happiness of her tongue between my teeth, her breast beneath my hand.

Gradually, as if testing itself, my sex swelled—a new muscle feeling its way. It was pressed between our bellies as if to keep it from harm. It felt like something separate from me, a visitor.

When Chris slipped it into her I knew that "it" was me. I was glad to feel how wet she was and to know that she was truly pleased. As I entered her smooth slippery hidden recess, I grunted with pleasure. This was a feeling I had completely forgotten. Chris sighed at the same time. It seemed to me that entering a woman's penetralia was the best feeling a man could have, that it was so completely satisfying in itself that it alone could suffice as the sex act, this simply going in and being received.

It's true I'd forgotten about the other parts, and they are pretty nifty, too, pretty outstanding in the realm of human feeling, but when you're having an orgasm, you're not as aware of yourself and your lover as you are at that exquisite moment of entry, a moment which to me assumes the proportions of an epiphany.

An orgasm, on the other hand, is essentially a fit. A seizure is what it amounts to. So instead of that previous intense awareness, you have instead a misplacing of yourself. Your ego disappears. In most cases, such as in going mad, losing your ego is terrifying, but orgasm is just brief enough to have the terror turn to exaltation. Your body is imprisoned in an astounding experience which your mind can't enter to participate in and wreck.

Just as if you were dropped off a cliff. Your body would be so busy getting ready for the landing that your mind would be left behind. And who needs it? It would be useless and also embarrassed to be there.

I'm sorry to say that I fell asleep about thirty seconds after our consummation, which wasn't very gentlemanly, but Chris told me later that she cradled me in her arms, feeling happy and honored, and was just as glad not to have to talk.

"You look like a boy," she said upon my wakening. "All your wrinkles have smoothed away."

"Happily my beard covers a multitude of them. Now, if I could just grow my eyebrows."

Chris giggled.

"My beamish Chris, don't you think we should broach a bottle of champagne in honor of this occasion? We have been through a lot together, you and I. You stood by me when I fled and hid, never asking or judging."

"You stood by me the same way, through my pregnancy and birth."

"I hope you don't feel I abandoned you by sending you home."

"No, my Muir. You did the right and necessary thing. It was good for me and Laurie to be here in Inverness. But not a day went by that I didn't think about you and long to be in your presence, just be in the same room as you." She paused and sat up, stretching happily. "How about that champagne? Let's go back to the garden and have it there. It's so pretty."

"I'll meet you there presently."

When I had showered, dressed, gone to the cellar for the champagne that I knew would be there, and brought it to the garden, Buster was just coming through the gate.

"Welcome home, Mr. Scott."

"Thank you, Buster. I recollect you were instrumental in getting me here. You might say," I explained to Chris, "he insulted me home."

"Will you join us in some champagne, Buster?" Chris asked.

"Sure. You bet."

"I'll get another glass." Chris went to the house.

"Buster, I understand I have you to thank for keeping the garden so beautiful. I would like to pay you for your time spent."

Buster flushed. "Well, let's see, five years at five dollars an hour, I suppose that's about fifty thousand dollars. I'll take a check."

There was a snort of laughter and I saw that Masefield had entered the garden and was leaning against the wall, listening.

"Hi, Masefield," Buster said.

"Don't let me interrupt this noble restitution," Masefield said.

Chris returned to the garden, then wheeled around muttering about one more glass.

"I'm sorry if I insulted you by offering to pay," I said, a little stiffly. "I would like to know why you put so much time and energy into it, however. Surely not for Sunny. She wouldn't care."

"Well, when Sunny got back from Paris she sort of howled when she saw the garden was all dry, so I watered it for her and then I just kept on keeping it watered, then weeded, then planted. The years went by. I liked doing it."

This was all very unconvincing. Much as it pained me, I had to go on with it. "Masefield will tell you that when I saw this garden upon my return, my first thought was that Andy had been here."

"Andy who?" Buster asked annoyingly.

"Andy, my son," I barked. Then I coughed into my hand as if to show that I hadn't really barked but had been taken by a coughing spasm.

"You remember," Masefield reminded him, since, after all, Buster had been away for a while, "the Andy Sunny's mom's been looking for yea these many years."

There was something in Masefield's tone that was annoying too, something different. Maybe I was being too sensitive.

"Oh, that Andy," said Buster.

"Buster," I said, the words flying from my mouth thoughtlessly, "it seems that you purposely try to infuriate me, or else you really are dumb—in which case you couldn't possibly be Andy."

"I'm not Andy," Buster said. "Don't worry."

"Do you remember, in Lanesville, when I thought you were me?"

"No."

This was outrageous. He was purposely not remembering.

Chris had now rejoined us and was opening the champagne and pouring the four glasses. It wasn't being much of a celebration, but she didn't seem to notice the conflict in the air.

Masefield, looking intrigued, moved away from the wall and drew closer to me and Buster.

"You had just arrived on your bicycle," I persisted. "I was coming up the path from the rocks. I looked up and saw you and thought you were me when I was young. If you *are* Andy, you would look like me when I was young. You don't look that way now, here. But in that instant, in the distance, I definitely thought you were me."

"Mr. Scott, I am not you when you were young and I am not your dead son, Andy. Also, you did not think that when you saw me in Lanesville. What you thought was that you were your father."

"This is a crazy conversation," Chris said, coming closer and handing around the champagne.

"Not at all," said Masefield. "This is your typical everyday Inverness conversation."

I felt extremely abashed, because Buster was right. I had distorted my perceptions of that Lanesville day. "You're right," I credited him. "But now I realize that the reason I thought I was my father was because of you looking so much like me when I was young."

"Even though I don't look that way to you now."

"Right. You don't now because I know that you are Buster. But then, when you had suddenly appeared out of the blue unexpectedly, I didn't have my knowledge of you as Buster to get in the way of my first impression, which was that—"

"Don't say it again, sir," Masefield suggested rather pleadingly. "You're getting overwrought."

"That you were me," I finished anyhow, finished lamely, feeling that Chris was correct in calling this a crazy conversation, one that surely had gone on long enough. "When I was young," I added, completing the thought, unable to help myself.

"I am not you when you were young," Buster repeated, as if he were making a formal statement to the press. Apparently he had decided to be infuriating again and make a fool of me in front of Masefield and my lover.

I became hopelessly angry at his treatment of me. I lost my temper, saying (shouting), "Right! And you are not Andy, who would have grown into a flower of young manhood with a soaring intelligence and amazing charisma. He would have been like Masefield, only more so, not at all like you, who are a clod, a moronic clod. To even suggest that you are my Andy is to defile the legend."

I staggered a little and sat down, heaving a great sigh that was more like a groan. Unaccustomed as I am to raising my voice— fighting was what it amounted to—and that on top of an unaccustomed epiphany and seizure, I was definitely overdoing it and felt exhausted.

As well, I was extremely embarrassed at my behavior, and yet I believe I was provoked. I defy Masefield or Buster himself to tell me I was not provoked.

Meanwhile, Buster flushed brightly at my words, which I admit were unduly harsh, and yet he did not grow angry in return. In fact, to my astonishment, he grinned and said, "Good. I want to be my own legend. I want to be the legend of Buster."

"To Buster!" Masefield raised his glass and drank.

"Yes, to Buster!" Chris said, drinking. "And to Muir's homecoming. And to us all." She looked around. "Where in heck is Sunny? Has she gone back to sleep?"

"She's at work," said Masefield. "Someone around here has to work and support us, especially since Buster just blew off his fifty thousand."

"Buster, I apologize," I began.

"Forget it." Then he had the temerity to lean down to where I sat and kiss me on the mouth, obviously meaning to anger and infuriate me again. Temerity was it? Or was it incredible generosity of spirit such as Andy would have had or such as Buster himself did in fact now have and that I as a young man, or old man, didn't?

"I want to say, as a flower of young manhood—" Masefield began.

"Is no one to show me any respect?" I complained.

"Certainly not. You yourself have written that respect is an odious thing to show anyone. It isn't good for them."

"I am about to write another book, a last book, refuting all my former writings. Chris is going to help me."

She came over to where I sat and I put an arm around her waist. "Also, we are going to live together and be sweethearts."

We all drank to that and finally got a proper celebration going for poor Chris. In due course Masefield went to the cellar for more bottles.

# 31. LOCKING IN DADDY

Everyone had been on my case about sleeping so much, coming to the water house at all times of day and night to roust me out of bed and lecture me, as if you could fake a concussion for God's sake, and now here I find them, all four of them, snoozing away in the garden, when I arrived around five o'clock. It was like a spell had been cast by a confused fairy.

Four empty bottles of champagne attested to the fact that it was not a spell. Buster and Chris could scarcely handle two sips let alone a full glass, so Masefield and Daddy must have done the main damage.

They were a huddle of bodies on a grassy hummock in the middle of the garden on which the day's last hour of sun was still lingering. Their various heads lay in each other's laps, Daddy's hand rested on Chris's hair like a bird in a nest, and Buster and Masefield were sort of twined together as if they'd fallen asleep in the middle of a wrestling match.

They all looked so adorable, I wanted, in true fairy-tale tradition, to wake each one with a kiss, but I figured I'd be more effective if I went into the kitchen and slammed around making coffee.

I went into the house, which was already looking much better, stacks of books having materialized as well as vases of flowers.

My coffee making did the trick, and one by one they came in, looking sheepish, as drunkards and idlers can't help but look in the uncompromising presence of a working woman still in uniform such as myself.

"Where are the kids?" Chris asked through the steam of her coffee.

"At a birthday party. Look, you guys," I said to Chris, Masefield, and Buster, "you've all heard about my big realization that I had when I thought I'd lost M, but now I've got to tell Daddy so if you don't want to hear it again . . ."

"Please don't tell it," Chris said, shakily setting her coffee mug down on the counter and turning a pleading face toward me.

"What?" Nobody had ever told me not to tell my realizations, nobody I loved, anyhow. I was so amazed. "Why?"

"You'll ruin everything." She leaned toward me, holding out her hands as if making an offering. It was not at all like Chris, who tended to yell if she wanted something. The three men were sort of standing around us with their faces hanging out, maybe still half-asleep or still drunk. Masefield looked pretty haggard.

"Muir's mind is at peace now," Chris said. "He's even ready to write again. We love each other and are going to live together, and if you start giving him a big sob story about your mother, he'll get all upset and the good work of these years away from her will be undone."

This was pretty big news about their living together, but all I could do was stammer, "S-s-sob story?"

"Yes!" Chris was getting back in stride now and starting to yell. "You're just romanticizing her looniness. Fuck your big realization."

"Chris, is this you speaking? My buddy? My backer in all that I do and think? You know how Mom has been my main concern."

"Well, it's time you felt some concern for your immediate family. And your friends."

"Calm down now, Chris," Daddy said, putting his arm around her. "I have to hear it. Nothing Sunny says will change what we've planned and I am perfectly in command of myself."

"Yes, let her tell it," Masefield said. "*Again.* I've only heard it fifteen times so far and it's possible I missed some of the finer points."

I sent him a stricken look. This was the man who wooed me by saying he thought repetition enhanced and enriched the facts.

He came over to me and pressed his cheek to mine, whispering, "Let it go."

What in heck was going on here?

Now Buster spoke. "I agree with Chris. There's nothing to be gained by mentioning it."

They were all against me. Was it because of Chris and Daddy getting together? Were they right that I should clam up?

"Anyhow, Sunny," Buster continued, "why suppose that what you felt about M and me duplicates Mom's feelings at the time of what's-his-name's loss?"

"What's-his-name? Why do you say what's-his-name?" I asked Buster, all amazed.

"He says it to annoy," Muir said grimly. "And I insist on hearing your realization."

"I'll be brief," I said with a haughty glance to Masefield for his belittling attitude regarding my repetition and one to Buster for not giving it credence. "When we lost little M that afternoon on the bay, I was of course unconscious at the time. When I awoke at the hospital and was told that he was lost and not yet found, floating somewhere in the cold waters of the night, I have to admit my first thought was for Buster. I knew the loss of little M would be hard on me, but what I would not be able to endure would be Buster's grief, for he had left M in my care, M, his treasure, the light of his life, and I had lost him.

"I knew then that Mom's mad grief was not just at having lost Andy, but it was feeling to blame for causing you, Daddy, such suffering. All these years she had not just been looking for Andy; she had been looking for Andy for you."

Daddy sat down in a chair, not in perfect command of himself one bit. His face seemed to collapse. His eyes and mouth were open as if drinking in some nourishing sight that might save him at the last minute. It scared me.

I saw that in my haste and need to tell him, not heeding the warnings of my friends, I had not considered the effect my realization would have on him. Chris, more lovingly, had. Now I could see how it might look to her that I was anxious to hurt him, not help him. Was I? Was this my way of getting back at him for going away and hiding out?

"Yes, Sunny." He found his voice. "I believe you are right. It's possible that I have misunderstood her all these years. All she ever dreamed of was my happiness, and she would periodically go mad when she realized that unless she could find Andy for me, she could never achieve her dream."

He hung his head. "And then, at the last, I deserted her."

"See, see!" Chris shouted at me like a maniac. "Look at him. I knew this would happen."

She went to Daddy where he was sitting, bent over with her hands on his shoulders, and roughly shook him. She said, staring him in the eyes as if to burn the words into his brain, "You didn't desert her. She doesn't even know you left. 'Who will look after your father?' she asked Sunny. Right? Are those the words of a woman only wanting your happiness or of a woman sailing the bay and having a hell of a good time, a woman who's gone round the bend, granted, slipped her moorings, but one who's left it all behind, just like Bart has? Bart didn't want responsibility anymore, either. He bagged it and hit the road. Mom hit the water and doesn't care damn-all for either of you. She *never* cared two bits about Sunny and why she's Sunny's 'main concern' beats the hell out of me."

Why was she my main concern? Why should she be more important than those loved ones right here with me now?

"Chris," he responded. "I think what I must do is talk with Bart. I must clear everything up with Bart if you and I are to be together."

"No," I said. "He's dangerous. He's gunning for you. He's . . ." I started to say he was crazy, but what did that mean?

"I must talk with him." Daddy got up and put on his jacket,

apparently ready to set off that instant. "There is a lot to talk about and to think about. It's time I came wholly out of hiding." He sighed. "I don't want to."

"I'd advise against it, sir. Sunny's right." This from Masefield.

"He feels so bad that he wants to go looking for trouble. Thanks to Sunny and her 'main concern.'"

"Will you shut up about my 'main concern'?" I was beginning to lose my temper, but I knew I was mad at myself.

"I have to clear everything up," said Muir, tending to repeat himself in the spirit of his daughter. "It's time."

He paused and we all stood silent with the weight of the long sad story upon us. "What if," he suggested heavily, "what if Bart is right in saying that I killed this woman who only wanted my happiness?"

"Oh, Lord!" Chris sat down and buried her face in her hands. I couldn't blame her. Daddy had completely disregarded everything she'd said—if he'd even listened in the first place.

"There have been sightings!" said Buster, going into the sightings speech that he'd been giving me, and anyone else who doubted her existence, for the past five years. "By all the townspeople. Sunny herself has spoken with her. M was pulled out of the bay and saved by her."

"Yes, Buster." Muir sighed deeply. "Sightings indeed. Ghostly sightings. Now I will lay that poor ghost to rest." He held up his hand. "No one is to follow me."

We all looked at each other. Every last one of us was prepared to follow him.

"Sir . . ." Masefield spoke formally, almost archaically, in the way he often seemed to do with Daddy. "It is night and Bart is not easy to find even during the day. He lives in the fields and woods and the ditches alongside the road. It would be too painful for us all to have you roaming the roads looking for Bart as if yet another one of us had gone mad, and too desperately hard on Sunny. I beg you to wait for tomorrow and let me attend you in your search, attend and help you. I have spoken to the man myself, earlier this week. I know where he can be found."

I sent Masefield a look of gigantic gratitude for this speech, as indeed did Buster and Chris.

In fact, we all looked so grateful and relieved at each other that we didn't notice that Daddy paid no attention and kept moving toward the door.

Buster astonished us all by grabbing Daddy by both arms, which he pulled behind his back. But then Buster was always a man of action when you came right down to it.

"Ow!" howled Daddy.

Buster said to Masefield, "We'll just have to lock him up for the night."

"Unhand me!"

"You're right, Buster. But where?"

"His old study has a lock on the door," I said, enthusiastically becoming an aider and abettor in this violence on my father. "The key is in it."

Buster half dragged, half carried, the famous philosopher to the study.

"Get this moron away from me!" Daddy shouted. His face was no longer collapsed but ruddy with rage. I had never seen Daddy this way and I kind of liked it. He certainly had gotten a lot more expressive over the years of his hiding out. Of course I didn't like him calling Buster a moron, but I'd long ago given up on him appreciating Buster. Also, it *was* too bad that Buster had to refer to Andy as "what's-his-name."

"I'll go in with him," said Chris. Before she closed the door she looked daggers at me. "See what you've done," she hissed bitterly.

"Yes, I see," I said, looking the daggers back at her with some other weapons thrown in. I was through feeling bad and had come around to feeling I'd done right. "I had to do it and I'm glad I did. Daddy's right. It has to be cleared up." I suddenly had a flash of fury remembering how both she and Daddy had blithely left me with this whole problem of Mom. "You're both of the 'run away from trouble' school of thought, as is Buster, come to think of it. But I'm not. Nor is Masefield. We like to figure things out and do what has to be done."

She started to remonstrate and I slammed the door on her.

Masefield looked at me fondly and sort of shook his head.

"What did I run away from?" asked Buster, coming out of the

study a minute later and locking the door behind him with Chris and Daddy inside.

"Me. When Masefield came. If that wasn't running away, what was it?" For the first time (maybe because it was the first time I'd seen Buster since he got home when I was awake and on my feet), I realized (another realization) that I had a lot of anger in me (unreasonable though it may seem) for Buster leaving me and M.

In fact, right now, now that I was awake, I felt like I was angry at everyone.

"It wasn't running away, it was going away," Buster defended himself.

"You deserted me." I used Daddy's word.

"Maybe you're right. But one thing you're wrong about. I don't love M more than you. It is you who are my treasure and the light of my life. I would never have blamed you. Never. And I don't know if I believe that all Mom wanted was Muir's happiness, but I do know that's all I want for you."

"What is happiness, Buster?" I demanded rather crabbily. "Tell me that."

"Being with people you love."

I looked at him with complete understanding because that's what I thought it was, too. It cheered me up. Someone around here knew what was what. "Then you were wrong to run away," I said.

"You're right," he said humbly. "I was wrong. It was unforgivable. I promise I will never leave you again as long as I live."

"That's good, Buster." It was. It made me glad. It was a good promise. "Then we'll always be a family."

Buster got such a look of happiness on his face that it's true he almost did look moronic. Then he creased his forehead. "Is it all right with Masefield if I never leave you again?"

Masefield was standing there listening to the whole thing and Buster looked at him, too, as he asked me.

"Yes," I said. "Wouldn't it be all right, Masefield?"

"Not if it would wound Buster afresh every time I came back."

This was the first time he had made an audible statement of his intent to leave me. It was like he'd laid off and punched me in the jaw. I staggered and fell back against the wall. He grasped both my arms, steadying me. "I will come back," he said to me gently, seeing my anguish. "I will. Often and often. But in between times, I will have to be going."

"But you won't stay? You won't ever stay?" I asked tremulously, knowing the answer, having known it all along, since the day he arrived. "Now? Or ever?"

Buster's face reflected my pain or, more likely, was his own pain in realizing at last and for certain how desperately I loved Masefield.

"No, Sunny. I can't stay. Happiness to me isn't just being with the person I love. It is . . . finding out."

"Finding out?" I gasped. The words were incomprehensible to me. I muffled a sob. "Finding out what?"

He thought a second and said, "Why the world wags and what wags it."

I didn't get it, but Buster did. He spread his arms and said, "But you can learn that here."

Masefield just laughed scornfully. "Oh, yes. The microcosm as opposed to the macrocosm, I suppose."

"Sort of," said Buster mildly.

Chris knocked and we let her out. She looked a lot happier. "I've arranged that I will go with Muir tomorrow to see Bart."

In unison we cried dauntingly, "That's idiotic! No!"

Masefield elaborated, "It will only enrage Bart more to see you both together."

"I've already figured I should go," Buster said. "Bart knows me and likes me pretty well. I can protect Muir from him if necessary."

"Muir is furious at you for 'manhandling him,' as he calls it." Chris giggled. "He never wants to see you again as long as he lives."

"Daddy sure has changed," I said. "He's so *emotional*. Are you still mad at me, Chris?"

"No. It's only that I waited so long to be with Muir, and to lose him again on the very day. . ." She began to look glum again and scared. "What if Bart somehow convinces him he did kill your Mom?"

"I think we should all go right now and kill Bart," I suggested, and meant it, too. Everyone else seemed to consider the idea in the light of it being a perfect solution.

"I think, instead, we should all stay with him now in his study so he won't feel locked out as well as locked in," Masefield said, unlocking the door.

We didn't stay in there with him because he was gone. Out the window, of course, what could be simpler? We heard the car start. It emerged that we all had walked over so Daddy had taken the only car. Something else emerged.

Chris, clutching her brow, asked, "Have you ever noticed that if your father asks you questions, you answer them no matter what?"

"Yes."

"Well, I told him all the different places Bart camps."

# 32. NOT RIGHT

I got out of my bag and it was colder than a sonofabitch. It was only 5:30 with the sun not up but the birds were fluting away like it was high noon and a posse of raccoons was climbing up after their nests. I put on my coat and tied a rope around the waist so the air wouldn't blow up the skirt. There was fog and the air was wet but that weren't nothing new.

I had some air left so I put some twigs on the coals, then sticks. Below me, where I could see under the fog, a herd of elk went by in their rocking-horse run from a copse of trees through a clearing and behind another copse. They just kept on coming like a string of beads, like they were going around, not by. Musta been a hundred of 'em.

I made my coffee and a mess of oatmeal and raisins that I'd eat hot and have the leftovers cold for lunch. After I ate and drank, I just sat and looked around for an hour or so.

That was the good time of day when I just sat and looked around, my breakfast still warm in my belly and no work to go to.

If I could have just sat on through the day and kept away from folks, but something always drove me to get up and go walking until I could talk to someone. Like I couldn't help it. I couldn't leave well enough alone and know when I was feeling good and stay that way. I got up and went out along the roads and collared people and talked to them, and the more I did that the more riled up I got because of their attitudes and their not understanding me. Some of 'em would be frightened of me. And some would sneer. And some would be pitying and I hated that worst of all.

I don't know why I didn't just keep on sitting and looking around and feeling peaceful. It weren't that I was lonely. How can you be lonely in all this nature where even a cloud's company? And nature never riles you. Even being cold as a sonofabitch is all right because then you make a fire and put something hot in your belly and that's good.

At night you can watch the fire until you sleep. You can watch the flames and listen to the hiss and pop of the burning sticks and other sounds, too—frogs, owls, the night insects— and that's all good, all of it, goddamn it. I wish I'd known it before. Though being a cowboy was good, too, damned good, and I could ride! Goddamn it but I could stay on a bucking bronco like my balls were glued to his back, and I could rope a steer so you'd think the rope had been magicked out of the air. And being a father was all right. I wouldn't have missed that for nothing. But that's when all the goddamn trouble started that I can't get rid of to this day because of the fucking philosopher who screwed everything for me and ruined my life!

I got up and started getting ready to walk because just thinking about that man made my brain freeze up and the only way to thaw it out was to talk it free. I had to tell someone about it, about how he ruined everything between me and my daughter, the only person who ever loved me. How he got her pregnant and killed his wife so he could take her away from her own father.

And I'm the one they sneer at and run away from—me, the father, not him, the murderer.

But for once I didn't have to go find someone to talk to because someone was walking toward me from the road where I saw he'd parked his car. I was pretty surprised to see such a thing as someone walking toward me. He was an old geezer, looked like, but at least he walked like a man used to walking and not just on sidewalks.

"Howdy," he said, stopping about ten feet away.

I looked him over, glaring a little. It was damned peculiar, his parking his car and walking over to my fire like that, like he owned the place and was going to throw me off.

"What the hell do you want?" I tried him with. "I got a right to be here."

"To talk. Just to talk. Any more coffee in that pot?"

Who the fuck did he think he was, marching over and asking for coffee? Anyways there weren't no more.

I glared at him good. "Talk about what?"

"Whether or not Muir Scott killed his wife."

He knew my topic all right.

"You're the second person's come to me this week. Some snot-nosed city kid came around wanting to hear my story. Said he was investigating, but he weren't no one with the sheriff's department—I know all a them assholes."

Even I didn't give him coffee, he sat down anyways, grunting a little as he did it, and looked at me through these thick glasses. He weren't as old as I figured. It was the gray beard made him seem he was. I held the silence a while to see if he could take it and he did. In fact, he seemed so comfortable not talking I began to worry that unless I said something a couple of days would go by. So I started talking, and like always it was a relief to me.

"This Muir Scott took my daughter from me when she was just a kid. He had a big house and lots of money and he gave her any damn thing she wanted. People came from all over hell and gone to see the fucker and it impressed her what a bigshot he was. Nobody ever come to my house to look at me and I wouldn't want them to, neither.

"He turned her against her own father. Far as I know he fucked her too. She got into his clutches. She thought he was God. I lost her. She was as good as dead to me, only worse because she was alive and scorned me, looked at me like I was dirt, comparing me to him."

"I lost a son," the man said. "Losing a child can make you crazy."

"I feel like I'm crazy sometimes. I feel like I'm going berserk whenever I think about him and what he did. But most times I feel like I'm the only sane one because I'm the one that knows."

"Grieving can confuse you, make you imagine things."

"I don't imagine nothing. I know what I saw with my own eyes."

"Grieving made me shut down," he said.

"Shut down? Is that anything like shutting up?" I asked, wishing he would so I could get on with it.

"My feelings . . ."

"I don't give a shit about your feelings," I said because it griped me the way he kept horning in on my story. "I thought you wanted to hear *my* story. You keep trying to talk about yours."

"So it seems." He laughed a little. "Maybe I should hit the road like you did and tell my story to all and sundry. Trouble is, I'm not sure what my story is. And I forget things."

"Well, I don't forget nothing and I don't forgive nothing, either."

"What did you see?"

"Eh?"

"You said you know what you saw."

"I seen him scuttle the boat. Her one-design. He towed it out, rowing quiet, not using his outboard, and sank it to the bottom of the bay. Now why'd he do that if her body weren't in it too?"

He listened to me real hard, then sort of ate his lips and shook his head. "I don't know."

"And why'd he take off outa here later that night, never to be seen again, taking my daughter with him who was pregnant?"

"I don't know."

"And why don't the cops investigate? I'll tell you why. Because he tells his daughter her mother's out on the bay. And the daughter believes him so the cops do, too. Why would anybody believe a fucking idiotic lie like that? The daughter, maybe, but the cops? And the daughter still believing it five years later? Can you beat that?"

"But hasn't she been seen out there?"

"It's the daughter who's been seen looking for her, that's who's been seen. And anything else was a ghost because the murdered stay ghosts until justice is done, and I don't blame the poor dead bitch none, either. I'd haunt the hell out of a place if I was done in like she was."

"It's a terrible story. How I wish I knew if it were true. The fact that I know that some parts aren't gives me hope to doubt the rest, and yet... and yet..."

"So it's up to me to kill him and put the ghost to rest and get my daughter back and show the world what's right."

"Maybe *she* towed the boat out and sank it."

"Who?"

"Muir Scott's wife. Could it have been she?"

I got up, beginning to feel agitated and having to walk even if it was in circles. "I tell you I seen him with my own eyes!"

"It was night."

"Fuck the night!" I screamed at him. "I know what I saw!"

He stood up and grabbed my sleeve so as to still me. He said, "I am he."

"He? Who? What the hell kind of English is that—I am he? Who the hell are you, anyways?" I pulled away from him and started waving my arms, flapping them up and down like a vulture trying to raise up from a carcass after it's stuffed itself. I screamed at him, "What do ya mean coming over to my camp and interrogating me? What do ya want with me?"

He tried to grab ahold of me again, but I was walking around and didn't want to look at him no more.

"I am Muir Scott and I want to clear this matter up."

"The hell you say."

"I am Muir Scott."

"Get outa here!" I shouted, commencing to flap my arms some more. "Go on. Git! Git! Git!"

He left, walked slowly across the field back to his car.

I sat down and put my face in my hands and rocked back and forth, back and forth, making sounds, moaning sounds. It's not right, I thought. It's not right. It's not right.

# 33. THE BLUE HILL

The morning after trying to lock in Muir, we all had breakfast together in Muir's house, where we'd spent the night after getting someone to bring the kids over, and then Sunny went off to the P.O., Chris and Masefield went looking for Muir, and I hung around waiting for the fog to lift so I could go get M out of school and take him to see the bright blue hill.

I'd come across it a few days before when I was bicycling around looking for some little rental to turn into a combination living space and bike shop. I'd turned off the road and started to go cross-country, which these special wheels I made for my bike allowed me to do, and when I rounded a blind curve in this gulch, I came upon a hill that was all blue with wild lupine flowers. The year before there'd been a burn on that hill and the lupine had all reseeded before the grass could take hold, so it was pure blue. It made you feel like you should look up and see a green sky or look over and see a pink ocean. It made you gasp. It made you feel religious. It made you feel like screaming for joy, which is what M did when he saw it, screamed for joy.

A scream is the one sound man makes without thinking first, not being able to help himself. The one involuntary sound. It's a good one.

Maybe a gasp is involuntary, too, but it isn't a sound so much as a sudden altered breath. A sob is not involuntary because sobs you can decide about.

M and I went to the top of the hill and lay down together, bodies straight, arms hugging tight, and then we rolled down the hill, side over side, like we were one person, and the crushed flowers made the air so sweet we pretended the lupine scent was a drug that made us crazy. That way we could spend about an hour just being silly and acting all idiotic, seeing who could be the biggest idiot on the big blue hill. M won.

Then I took him to this little rust-colored house I'd found vacant. It was pretty ugly but it was sturdy. It had integrity. It had a good brick chimney. We couldn't see into it because it was all shuttered. There were a lot of little pink fluffy roses growing all over it.

"Imagine it painted white, M."

"Or blue!"

"You've got blue on the brain." I walked over to another building. "Now look here, see this garage." It had double doors held together by a busted padlock so I swung one of them open, giving it a shove when it got caught in the long wild grasses. "This will be the bike shop. It's a good big space and it has windows for fresh air. It's near enough to town that people could find me but not so near they'd hang around bothering me all day so I couldn't get the bikes built. We'd have to put in electricity and some kind of heat. Maybe we don't need heat."

"We don't need heat," M said. "Well, maybe a little heat."

"Here in this shop"—I was already imagining my tools hung up neatly, each in its proper place, and the machinery all in a row on the cement floor, and the bike bodies hanging from the ceiling, over there the wheels—"we're going to build a bike like the world's never seen. The world will be astounded, M, when they see this bike we build, although it's not good to brag, of course."

"Did you draw some pictures of it?"

"No, but I will. I'll draw you some pictures of it when we get back. That's a good idea. I should have pictures on paper as well as in my head. I've got a whole bunch of them in my head." I smiled. I felt happy. Yes I felt happy, even though I knew for certain now that Sunny didn't love me, would never love me in the way I hoped and dreamed and always believed she would. But it was all right because I had M and the bike shop and all this beauty everywhere you looked, like the blue hill, the pink ocean. I was so lucky, so lucky.

I felt little M's hand in mine. "Buster, what's wrong? Why are you crying?"

"Oh, shucks, M, I don't know. I'm sorry. I just wish—" I sobbed and wiped my eyes and nose on the sleeve of the arm M wasn't holding. "I just wish we could all be together. I shouldn't be saying it to you, I suppose, because you're just a little kid and it's hard to understand, but I love Sunny so much and the thing is people just can't help who they love and don't love, can they? You can't make yourself feel something you don't feel."

"Mom wanted me to try to love Masefield, but I didn't even want to try. Still, I'm getting to *like* him a little."

"That's good."

"Buster?"

"What?"

"Mom missed you a lot. She always made me tell her every single word you said when you called."

"Don't give me hope, M. I've got to stop hoping. For years I didn't. I kept believing the day would come when she'd want to marry me. Even when Masefield came, even when I was away, I believed right up until last night when I finally saw how it was for her."

"How what was?"

"How much she loves him, how passionately..."

My chin hit my chest. I finished the sentence to myself: and, now, even for you, M, even for the bike shop, life just doesn't seem worth living when there isn't even any hope. Or any use. Before, Sunny at least needed me. She was all alone in the world, deserted by everyone. Now, everyone's back. And she's all grown up now too, a postmaster, a mother. She doesn't need me. And she never wanted me.

"Mom told me she wouldn't have woken up if you hadn't of come back and woken her up. She said you lied down on her hospital bed and talked her awake and that's how she got to find out I was alive."

"Come on, M, stop." I had to smile in spite of myself because he was being so cute trying to make me feel better.

"And when you went away she kept going to the door all hours of the day and night thinking you'd come back."

I laughed. I sort of laughed and sobbed at the same time. "Now you're making things up. Now you're really trying to trick your old Buster."

"It's true! Mom loves you best of all. Mom hates that old Masefield and I do, too."

"No, don't say that, M. He's a good man. I like him. He's all right. But I appreciate your trying to cheer me up. Come on, help me push this door shut and we'll get on home."

"Are you going to stop being a baby chicken?"

"I'm not being a baby chicken."

"You are, too."

"There's nothing wrong with crying. Don't ever let me hear that you got sad sometime and didn't cry."

"Well, what *is* being a baby chicken?"

"It's being scared or weak or being sorry for yourself. It's not trying. It's when you don't even try."

"Oh."

"Being a baby chicken is not allowed in this family."

"Because we're champions."

"That's right."

"But Buster, sometimes it's hard to know why you're crying. Whether you're really sad or just being a baby chicken about it."

"You get so you can tell."

"That's good."

When we got back to the water house, I looked through the porthole window before we went in and I saw Masefield and Sunny, just their heads, and it about gave me a heart attack. Their heads were sort of together, their brows bent toward each other almost touching, and on their faces were looks of the most terrible anguish, grimaces, really, and their faces looked wet,

Masefield's eyes were wide open seemingly full of tears and Sunny's were closed. I threw open the door all alarmed, thinking some terrible new sorrow had come on them and on us all, but no . . . no, they were arm wrestling.

# 34. BUSTER

Buster made me so mad. He burst in like a madman and naturally I lost my concentration and Masefield dropped my arm to the table. "It doesn't count!" I shouted.

Masefield just smiled, stood up, and lit a cigarette.

"Masefield, you know I just lost because of Buster bursting in like a madman and disturbing me."

"He didn't disturb *me*," he pointed out, and I had to admit he had something there. But he was a spy and I was a postmaster. Spies train themselves not to be disturbed.

"I'm sorry, Sunny," Buster said.

"Masefield," I pointed out, "this was a test of strength, not a test of who wouldn't be thrown off by Buster bursting in."

Masefield didn't deign to respond.

"I'm sorry," Buster kept saying.

"You probably *arranged* to have him burst in," I accused Masefield, who just smiled maddeningly through his smoke, the cigarette between his lips moving with his smile.

"I'm sorry, Sunny," Buster said.

"Mom, I'm going to make a peanut butter and jelly sandwich, okay?"

"Okay."

"Then I'm going over to Laurie's, okay?"

"Okay."

"Is there any news from Muir?" Buster asked.

"Yes. He found Bart, talked with him, and came away from the meeting intact. He and Chris are on their way over here now with the details. How come you guys smell so good?"

Buster told me about the blue hill and the future bike shop, but I could tell he was feeling really down. I wished I could make him happy. I wished I could somehow let him know how I valued him above all others, that all my years of waiting and looking—for Masefield, Daddy, Mom—were wasted because I'd had the best of all right beside me the whole time, him, Buster.

Beside me. That was the thing. I loved to have him beside me, night and day. It was so comfortable, so right. As if we were one person, thinking the same thoughts, hardly any need to voice them, our hearts beating steadily together, thump, thump, thump, our personalities in harmony, no discord.

But if I told Buster all this, he would say, Why don't you marry me, then? and I would have to say that I was hopelessly in love with Masefield and I couldn't help it.

Why can't I help it? I looked at Masefield, who had such a grappling hook on my heart, sprawling on the bed now in all his elegant length, half listening to Buster and thinking who knew what other thoughts on his own. I never knew what he was thinking and I always wanted to know. Masefield had mystery. He had humor, charm, such charm.

And he had ambition. He was going away again. Soon.

Could I help it? Maybe I could. What if I made up my mind to love Buster, the best man who ever lived, and totally forget Masefield?

My heart sank at the thought, and life here, even in all its known richness of Buster's love and friends and children and sailing and my good job and Daddy home, appeared bleaker than the moon, bleaker than the moon's moon, if there was such a place. I knew that waiting for Masefield, even for another five years, even all by myself, was better than no Masefield at all ever again.

"Hi, Mr. Scott," little M greeted his grandfather, who was coming in the door as he was going out. It shocked me and I shouted at him, "That's rude, M. Call him Grandpa."

"I don't want to. Anyhow, he's not my grandpa." M grabbed Laurie, who was coming in behind Muir with Chris, and they went running off down the pier.

"What in heck does M mean, Daddy's not his grandpa?" I wondered aloud.

"He probably thinks Buster is his *real* grandfather as well as his real father," Masefield said, standing up to greet them and then resuming his place on the bed.

There was a flurry of greetings all around as Daddy settled down and started telling about his dawn meeting with Bart. He described coming upon Bart at his campsite, then got to the heart of the matter.

"When I told him who I was, he couldn't take it in. When I repeated that I was Muir Scott, he became extremely agitated. I could tell that he wasn't willing to give up his litany, that he would be lost without his grievance, that he couldn't abide the notion of having to actually do something about me. He chased me away and I went."

Chris was sitting by Daddy on the wicker settee, and I went to sit on the other side of him. Buster stood by the window looking out. "He is a very unhappy man," Muir said. "Very unhappy indeed. I turned in on myself when Andy died and in place of my own persona erected that of the famous philosopher, the wise man, which, in truth, was only the guise of a crazy man, just as Bart has his guise of the wandering tale teller, the berserk Indian cowboy wronged by a bigshot."

I realized that Daddy was talking like a man to whom all had come clear—or almost.

"My guise was perfectly acceptable in society, even honored. His is deplored.

"Even my ignominious disappearance these last five years, wherein I sought to discover my true self, has only added to my reputation in the world."

He wasn't talking to us as much as himself. He seemed to have a new vigor to him.

"Whereas everything Bart does only causes him to be more reviled.

"In a way I envy him."

He fell silent then and seemed to ponder.

"The main thing is that you came out of it alive," Chris said a little nervously, not seeming to have followed any of this too well. I was having a little trouble myself. "You really frightened us all going off like that in the night."

But Daddy still hadn't finished. "We both of us went crazy rather than accept responsibility for our actions and omissions, for our behavior and emotions. I blamed Sunny's mother for what I conceived to be my miserable existence. He blamed me. Neither of us was prepared to blame ourselves."

I understood that all right. You can't blame other people and you can't depend on other people, either. You have to make your own life and be your own self. "I have to admit I'm surprised," I said. "I was convinced Bart would do you in."

"Don't let it make you give up having realizations," Masefield said. "That would be a terrible loss to us all."

"I think I'm having a realization now that I hate you," I responded.

Masefield laughed.

Suddenly he sprang to his feet from his lying-down position. Bart had entered. He was carrying a rifle.

Masefield, dressed in khakis and T-shirt, was not armed. His gun was in his jacket pocket. His jacket was hanging over the chair near to where I stood. My heart in my throat, I sidled in that direction.

"Bart, no!" This from Chris. "Dad, please . . ."

"Stand back, all a you." He gestured at us with the rifle. "Move closer together."

He was having trouble keeping an eye on all five of us, so I reached into the pocket, drew out the gun, and held it in my hands behind my back. Masefield saw and started easing my way.

This is how we were standing: Bart had come over and was in front of the window that overlooked the bay.

Facing him, in a row, was: Chris, Daddy, Buster, me—and Masefield was almost beside me.

"I got the law on my side," Bart said.

He smelled awful and looked wilder than ever. The adrenaline was rushing through my body like a tidal wave. All my hatred for Bart and all the misery he'd put me through flashed through my mind. I released the safety on the gun and was getting ready to blast away at him when I felt Masefield take it from me. Damn!

Bart said, "I been telling everybody I was going to do this and I am. It's only right. He's a murderer and justice will be done right now by the man he wronged and made a mock of."

"Listen to me, Bart," said Masefield. "You're making a big mistake and you'll get yourself in serious trouble."

Bart flickered his eyes over to him. "I remember you—the slick talker from the city. Well, I ain't listening."

"You'd better because Mrs. Scott is alive. That is common knowledge now since the recent sailing accident with Sunny's son, which I'm sure you've heard about. Sunny was knocked unconscious, and while I was saving her, little M, as he's called, drifted off out of sight. It was Sunny's mother, Muir Scott's wife, who found him, saved him, put him ashore. The boy himself saw her, talked to her, touched her."

"Bullshit!"

"No, Bart, not bullshit. If you'll look out at the bay now, just turn your head slightly, none of us will move, you will see her. She's out there now, sailing by in her one-design."

She was. We none of us did move. We were frozen into immobility as we looked out and saw Mom, sailing by, close by, and it was her as sure as I'm me. My heart filled with wonder and gladness. Daddy's face was agape but also relieved and glad, and Chris looked astounded. Only Buster seemed comparatively unmoved.

And Bart, who claimed not to see her.

He looked out briefly, turned back to us, said, "I don't see nothin'," and fired at Daddy.

Instantly, Masefield fired at Bart, a heart shot, but it was too late because by then Buster, who, at Bart's words, had stepped in front of Daddy, was down on the floor, having taken Daddy's bullet for himself.

Buster looked at me. He seemed to put everything he had, all that was Buster, all that he felt for me, in that last look, and then, then he wasn't there anymore, it wasn't Buster looking out at me, it was just eyes.

# 35. THE LEGEND OF BUSTER

$A$t the memorial service for Buster, a week later, I was the only one of all his friends, all his countless friends, who was unable to get up and say a few words. I just couldn't. I was still choked. I just hadn't been able to stop crying since he looked his last at me, and I wept all during the service, too. Yes, the tears just kept on producing themselves.

Forgive me for not speaking, Buster. You know I loved you more than anybody else did except maybe M. I hope you do. Oh, God, I hope you realized how much I loved you.

Deep down I knew he didn't. He didn't know or he'd still be here.

Or maybe he did know how much—exactly—and it was too little.

I would never, never be able to make it right.

I was so proud of, and grateful to, Masefield because he, who knew Buster the shortest time of all, gave the most wonderful eulogy.

"Here we've all come together to praise Buster," Masefield said. "And we're going to put a fine stone on his resting place, too, so he'll never be forgotten even by those who come after us. And we'll keep telling his story, each in our own way, so his legend will stay and will grow, the legend of Buster, which was a thing he wanted. He didn't want to be forgotten.

"I'm a stranger here in Inverness and I knew him least of all. In fact, I only knew him for the last ten days. But we're deeply connected because we both loved the same woman, Sunny Scott, and we have the same son, Masefield Scott.

"Here's what I know about Buster. He was an orphan boy who came into the care of Mama Clausen, now deceased, when he was five. He was mute. We'll never know what turned him mute or how he spent those first five years. He didn't speak for two years and then he spoke because he got an idea he wanted to tell about. He kept on speaking after that and he kept on getting ideas too. When he was a teenager he was a champion motorcycle rider, which shows he was a great athlete, a man of strength and courage. He didn't finish high school, but that doesn't show anything about how smart and original he was. He gave up his motorcycling when his baby was born, for safety's sake, and then he got very interested in bicycling. He loved Sunny since she was seventeen years old. He loved her so much that all he wanted was her happiness. He was father to her baby by another man, and when that other man came back to Sunny, Buster pedaled out of town and all the hell the way across the country so she could be with her lover.

"Buster returned to Inverness the instant he heard Sunny was in trouble. He arrived in time to give his life to save her father, a man who had never particularly admired him.

"As he died, he looked full at Sunny as if he were trying to take the vision of her with him to eternity. I hope he did.

"Buster was a man of immense kindness, full of love, a family man who never had a family of his own. All my life I have been looking for a superior human, a person who would possess intelligence, strength, and soul to a high degree. Naively, I even had a list of names of people to seek out because I thought they might fill the bill.

"To my surprise it turned out that Buster was the superior human being I sought. I was surprised because he turned out to be such a *human* human, which was something I somehow hadn't expected. I will never forget him or stop telling about him."

The last speaker was M. We were sitting around, about fifty of us, in the garden Buster had kept alive for Mom.

M stood up and still looked so little. He must have felt so, too, because he went and climbed this little hummock that Buster, or probably he and Buster together, had formed by the roses.

M simply said, "Buster was afraid of the water. One night he had to get across the water so I could be born and he went into it, scared to death, and even swam in it so as to get to Mom in time, and he got there, and then I was able to get born. He was my daddy."

# 36. LOOKING FOR BUSTER

I took a plant and some gardening tools to Buster's grave. Every time I came home I brought a plant that I thought would last pretty well, and it was getting to be quite an unusual garden around the stone. The gravesite was nice, on a high rise with the scent of the sea if not a view of it. I spent about an hour weeding and fertilizing and watering, and it made me feel good. I suppose I talked to Buster while I was at it. I always had to tell him the news, catch him up on what was happening with my life. I didn't talk aloud. It was a silent communion.

A voice interrupted. It was Laurie.

"Hi, Masefield. Sunny told me I'd find you here."

I stood up and looked down at her. As usual I felt awkward about hugging her. In any case my hands were too dirty and I sort of held them so she could see that they were. It wasn't that I wasn't happy to see her. I was.

"Hello, Laurie! I didn't know you'd be home. I was going to try to catch you in Berkeley on my way out of here."

"I heard you were coming, so naturally I hightailed it up to Inverness. You look great." She stood on tiptoe and, with her hands on my shoulders, kissed me on the cheek, which I bent down to her.

"So do you."

She did. I hadn't seen Laurie since Christmas and now it was September. She had one more year of college, but I had dropped out in the middle of sophomore year and now I just traveled around. She wore her usual jeans and sweatshirt outfit. After all her years of chubbiness she'd settled on being rather small and thin, but there was a sturdy quality to her as if you couldn't knock her over if you tried. She was very serious looking in the face, but I knew there was humor there and a lot of love.

"Masefield, every time I see you, I swear you've grown taller. What are you now, about six five?"

"About."

"And some of us still think of you as little M."

Laurie sat down on the ground, her arms hugging her knees. "Your dad came with you?"

"Yeah, we came together from Washington."

"So sometimes the president lets him get away."

"Hell"—I laughed, feeling proud—"he tells the president what to do."

"What's it like when Sunny comes to Washington? Have you ever been there at the same time?"

"Yes." I smiled. "It's like some great Indian chief of a century ago. She stands straight with her arms crossed, looks at everyone with contempt, and they're all cowed as hell. This is the woman who never went to college and barely passed the postal exam."

"I don't blame her for being contemptuous of this particular administration."

Laurie picked a piece of grass and, putting the blade between her thumbs, blew on it. It made a thin shrill sound. I wiped my hands on my pants and sat down beside her. Shoulders touching, we leaned against Buster's tombstone.

"Dad will probably come along to greet Buster, too, after he's been with Sunny a while," I said.

Laurie smiled and I knew she was thinking that "being with Sunny" meant being in bed, which is where they always went first thing when they got together.

"Every time I see your dad," Laurie said, "he talks to me to make sure I haven't forgotten Buster. The truth is that I don't remember him very well. It's so funny how much he cares about that even though he himself knew him so briefly."

"Sometimes I think he knew him best of all, understood something about him that the rest of us didn't. I remember Buster mostly as a wonderful presence but also, unfortunately, I remember clearest the sad days, the day he bicycled away and the day on the blue hill."

"I thought the blue hill was a really happy memory."

"It was."

I had never told anyone, not even Laurie, how he cried that day and told me Sunny didn't love him.

"It's hard to believe," I said, "that Buster would be in his forties now if he'd lived. Which he would have done if it hadn't been for Muir."

"You always say that. It makes me mad. I loved Muir," Laurie said defensively. "He was a good father to me and a good husband to my mom."

"I'm sure he killed Sunny's mom. That's something else Dad knows and isn't saying."

"M, they all *saw* Mom sail by that very moment of the shooting." She said it by rote. We'd been over it so many times over the years. She never looked at it fresh. Nobody did.

"Dad could make people see stuff."

"Right. Coins and fruit and stuff like that. *Not* a person sailing on the bay."

That was another thing I'd never told, that Dad had once shown me an image of Sunny sailing on the bay. It had been our secret that we'd never even mentioned to each other all these years. Of course, I hadn't been there at the shooting, but it always seemed to me it could have happened that Dad conjured up the image of Mom or hypnotized them into believing they saw her, succeeding with all except Bart.

"If she was dead," said Laurie, going on rotelike to the question she always asked, "then how do you explain her saving you, that story you told us all?"

"I can't explain it. Unless it was her ghost. And maybe it was her ghost they saw out the window that never appeared again because she thought it was Muir who was shot by Bart and therefore, avenged, she could go to her rest."

"Seems like a ghost, if there was even such a thing as a ghost, would know who was shot."

We both sat silent.

"Anyhow, I can't believe you're still so bitter after all this time, still blaming Muir."

"I'm not bitter," I protested. "It's just because we're here at the grave that I'm talking like this. I don't brood about it the whole time. It's only when I'm home I think of Buster and the whole story."

"That's good. Then try to remember that if it hadn't been for Buster giving his life, Muir never would have got to have written his last great book that put all his previous ones to shame, a book that really mattered to the world."

"Yeah," I responded, swallowing hard, "and the world never got to see the bicycle that Buster would have built."

I wiped my eyes on my sleeve.

"Oh, M," Laurie said feelingly.

"I don't just blame Muir," I told Laurie for the first time, maybe desperate to add something new to the exchange, "I blame Sunny, too. For not loving Buster enough. I think he wanted to die that day, that day of the blue hill."

We fell silent again. I realized I was spoiling our reunion.

Then Laurie said sadly, looking away, "A person can't help who they love."

I knew she was referring to her and me, how much she loved me and how I didn't return it in the way she needed.

Although I could see it was painful for her, it was good that she said it because it helped me, a little, to understand Sunny.

If I could love a woman, it would be Laurie.

"Laurie, you're such an idiot. We have this same conversation every time I come home."

She smiled and lightened up. "Speaking of being an idiot, M, isn't your father disappointed that you're not going back to college?"

"No. He doesn't care. Whatever I do or don't do, he seems to understand."

"It's funny you ended up loving him so much. More than Sunny, really, since it's he you decided to live with."

"Probably because I felt Dad loved me more than she did. Sunny can only love one person. And that one person is my dad. She loved him and she grieved for Buster and there wasn't any feeling left for me. I think..." Now it was my turn to say the painful thing, to look away when I said it. "I think she still grieves for Buster. I even think she goes looking for him the way her mom did for Andy."

Laurie put her hand over mine. "If so, M, I'll bet she's looking for Buster for you."